Readers are already raving about *Call Me Hope*, a powerful story about a young girl dealing with a verbally abusive mother:

"This beautiful, inspiring story should be read by mothers and daughters together. This captivating, healing novel brings extraordinary insight into the destructive emotional impact of verbal abuse on both mother and child. Together, with a promise and a pledge to one another, the gift of love is given."

—Ann S. Kelly, founder/executive director of Hands & Words Are Not For Hurting Project ®

"As an adult living in a verbally abusive relationship, I wish I'd known the subtleties of this insidious behavior years ago. *Call Me Hope* is a gift of insight and strength for children of all ages. Readers will now be able to identify the signs of verbal abuse and either survive in its midst or leave its grasp."

—Anonymous verbal abuse victim

"*Call Me Hope* is a beautiful story that captures how devastating verbal abuse is to a child's heart, mind, and soul. It is also an inspirational story of empowerment in which young readers learn the importance of reaching out to others when faced with difficult issues, which helps them cope, survive, and thrive. I highly recommend it!"

—Trudy Ludwig, children's advocate and bestselling author of *My Secret Bully*, *Just Kidding*, and *Sorry!*

"*Call Me Hope* introduces young readers to an amazing girl named Hope. Children who do not live in abusive homes may find her clever and creative. Those who DO live with the constant threat of abuse will surely find her inspirational."

—Pat Stanislaski, executive director of the New Jersey Task force on Child Abuse and Neglect, former executive director of the National Center for Assault Prevention

"A sensitive, heartrending book about parental verbal abuse and Hope's way of coping. Compassionately shared insight ending with promise for those involved. This book will be rewarding when shared with classroom discussion groups."

—Neva Huff, former educator

"Gretchen does a wonderful job of writing a hard story. I read this book aloud to twenty-five female inmates in jail, and they were captivated, as was I."

—Karen Rogers, Yamhill County Correctional Facility administrator

"A bittersweet *must-read* for every adolescent child and a powerful 'read-aloud' for those even younger. Gretchen has hit on a topic that is often very hidden from the world . . . verbal abuse. A remarkable story. . . As an educator for more than 30 years, I'm thrilled to see this issue faced head-on."

—Chris Morris, kindergarten teacher

call me HOPE

a novel by Gretchen Olson

Little, Brown and Company
Books for Young Readers
New York ❀ Boston

Also by Gretchen Olson:

Joyride

Little, Brown and Company

Hachette Book Group USA
237 Park Avenue, New York, NY 10017
Visit our Web site at www.lb-kids.com

First Paperback Edition: June 2008
First published in hardcover in April 2007 by Little, Brown and Company

The characters and events portrayed in this book are fictitious. Any similarity to real persons, living or dead, is coincidental and not intended by the author.

Library of Congress Cataloging-in-Publication Data

Olson, Gretchen.
   Call me hope / by Gretchen Olson—1st ed.
      p. cm.
   Summary: In Oregon, eleven-year-old Hope begins coping with her mother's verbal abuse by devising survival strategies for herself based on a history unit about the Holocaust, and meanwhile she works toward buying a pair of purple hiking boots by helping at a second-hand shop.
   HC ISBN: 978-0-316-01236-2 / PB ISBN: 978-0-316-01239-3
   [1. Child abuse—Fiction. 2. Mothers and daughters—Fiction. 3. Moneymaking projects—Fiction.
4. Schools—Fiction. 5. Stress (Physiology)—Fiction. 6. Oregon—Fiction.] I. Title.
   PZ7.O5185Cal 2007
   [Fic]—dc227   2006027896

HC: 10 9 8 7 6 5 4 3 2 1
PB: 10 9 8 7 6 5 4 3 2

RRD-C
Printed in the United States of America
The text was set in ITC Benguiat, and the display type is Day Dream.

For my Mother,
An *Angel Mom*
1923–1982

For children everywhere
suffering from verbal abuse,
I wish you courage.

"I will not use my hands or my words
for hurting myself or others."®*

Ann S. Kelly

*Official pledge of the International Hands & Words Are Not For Hurting Project®.
Ann S. Kelly, Founder and Executive Director.

CHAPTER 1

Role Models

The way I figure, good numbers are a good sign. Take the first day of 6th grade. Not only was it September 6, but I woke at exactly 6:06, which is lucky because it's perfectly balanced. Besides that, 6 is my favorite number. I kissed my fingers, touched the wall, and wished that 6th grade would be a great year.

Mr. Hudson looked over our class like he was figuring what kind of year he was going to have. Maybe he was looking for a good number, a lucky sign. He turned and wrote *role models* on the board, his bald spot bobbing along with his arm.

"What's the job of a role model?" he asked, turning back, wiping his hand on his pants.

My eyes shot down. I sucked in a deep breath. *Don't call on me. Please. Don't let sixth grade start with kids watching, waiting for an answer, remembering all the times I haven't paid attention.* I stared at my page of All-School Rules, the numbers and letters blurring. Rruulee ##1: BBeeSaafe.

"You have to be good for the little kids to see," answered Annette Stuckey.

Thank you, Annette.

"That's right." Mr. Hudson walked to the back of the room and took a sip of water from the fountain. "As sixth graders, you are now the oldest students at Eola Hills Grade School. You set examples for the rest of the school. Please take this responsibility seriously."

I slumped down in my chair. *You have to be good. You have to set examples. And — while you're at it — you have to be safe. Seriously. HA!* I crammed my pencil against the paper. *Snap!* The point flipped onto the desk, leaving flecks of black dust across Rule #2: Include Everyone.

Mr. Hudson cleared his throat. "I can't stress how important you are this year."

IMPORTANT. The pencil dust glowed and I brushed my rules clean. *Important.* I sat up tall and circled Rule #3: Be Respectful. Something fluttered in my chest. *Important.* My ears burned hot and my lips whispered a smile. I wrote across the top of my paper: 6 6 6 6 6 6 6 6 6 6 6 6 6 6 6 6 6 6 6 6 6 6 6

(In case you're wondering why 6 is my favorite number, take a look at the circle part. It's like you're going round and round, which is okay if you're a clock, but if you're a person you'll get dizzy and sick and you gotta get out. That's what the curvy top is for — escape — and you fly away from all the bad stuff to something perfectly wonderful.)

"So what's the best thing about sixth grade?" Mr. Hudson was wandering between our desks.

"OUTDOOR SCHOOL!" we shouted.

"You got it!" He gave us two thumbs-up. "That means 'Boom Chicka Boom.'"

"And rappelling," said Brody Brinkman.

"Creek walks!" someone shouted.

"Tie-dyeing." "Campfires." "Ooga Booga."

"And," said Mr. Hudson, bending to eye level, getting all mysterious, "rattlesnakes," he hissed.

A few kids squealed and protested, but mostly we tried to act cool. "Tastes like chicken," said Peter Monroe.

"So," said Mr. Hudson, standing and crossing his arms, "this is the year that's finally come, after all those jogathons and candy bar and magazine sales. The year you've been waiting for. The week you've been waiting for. Nights sleeping beneath the moon and stars, listening to the crickets and coyotes, and coming home with unforgettable memories." He smiled like he had those memories himself. "This is also the year to be on your best behavior and try your hardest. Come next spring," he said, tapping the wall calendar, "if we decide a sixth grader hasn't been a good role model, he or she might not attend Outdoor School."

My ears rang: *role model, role model.* My heart pounded: *I'm going. I'm going.* I outlined Rule #4: **Have Fun.** I checked my watch — 8:44. YES. A double number. I kissed my fingers and touched the table. *Please, God, let me be good — and have fun.*

Then I glanced at our last rule, #5: Problem Solve. My skipping heart screeched to a halt. There was no way the problems in my life would ever get solved.

CHAPTER 2

What's in a Name?

Here's a problem to solve: Names that rhyme. Like mine — Hope — which rhymes with *dope* and *mope*. My official name is Hope Marie Elliot. My mother picked Hope because it's a soap opera star's name and Marie for some singer, but Mom says I can't carry a tune to save my life. Sometimes Mom calls me Hopeless, which seems really weird. Does that mean I'm less than myself? Or not here at all?

My older brother, Tyler, calls me Hop, and if he wants my attention, it's HeyHop.

My father's name is Ryan Michael Elliot, but I don't know what he calls me. He never calls. Mom says he left us because I cried all the time when I was a baby.

I had colic: around-the-clock, 24-7 stomachache. Cry, cry, cry.

My mom's name is Darlene Delilah Elliot. Her big dream was to be an actress, but she had Tyler, then me (which she calls an accident), and then my dad left, so she couldn't go after her dream.

I'd rather be Hopeless than an accident, but that's another problem to solve.

Even though Mom didn't become an actress, she still thinks she's going to be discovered, so she wears lots of makeup and crazy clothes. For example: high-heeled boots with jeans and a sweater that's too small. She keeps her hair long, partway down her back, and colors it blond, plus she wears these huge gold earrings, which you'd think would pull her ears off. She tells everyone to call her "D.D."

Mom probably could be a great actress because she's always rehearsing, especially at school things like the annual carnival. Last year she volunteered to call out bingo. "B 8," she breathed into the microphone. "B as in 'bathing beauty.'" She gazed across the lunch tables, flipped her hair back, and smiled into an invisible camera.

Everyone thinks she's amazing to work full time and do decorations for the '50s Sock Hop and plan the Spring Fling Talent Show and raise two kids all by herself. A good actress name for her would be: "The Amazing D.D."

I'll tell you the worst name in all the world: *STUPID*. That word gives me one stinkin' stomachache, especially when Mom says it right in front of someone. For example: "Hope's been driving me nuts. She doesn't do anything I tell her. She's so *STUPID*."

By the time first grade arrived, Stupid Me was convinced I couldn't learn to read. But Mrs. Atkins was magical. She made sense out of all those alphabet letters and she made reading fun. Her book corner was piled with big pillows and stuffed animals and picture books with words I could figure out. And guess what? She read to her own kids every night. An Angel Mom.

I'll tell you my favorite name: Gabriela Feliciano. She's this amazing basketball player at Eola Hills High and her name's in the paper all the time. Doesn't it look pretty? All the high letters mixed with the low ones and the dots on all the *iii*'s looking like candles? It sounds pretty, too. Sometimes I say it out loud: *Gabriela Feliciano.* And, she's as beautiful as her name, with shiny, black, wavy hair pulled back from her face, plus thick, black eyebrows. The best part is she's always so happy. She has this big, glowy smile on her face. Even her dark eyes are happy. She probably doesn't have problems to solve. I bet no one calls her *STUPID.*

CHAPTER 3

Angels and Stars

"All those with blue eyes please stand." The *please* didn't soften Mr. Hudson's stone face. Chairs knocked and clanged as a bunch of Blue Eyes got up and glanced around at each other.

"This is just an experiment, but I want you to take it seriously and to focus on your reactions." Mr. Hudson took a piece of paper from his desk. "There are to be no comments as I read an announcement from the Yamhill County Commission on Youth Safety."

He cleared his throat. "From this day forward, no one with blue eyes may attend movies on the weekends, stay out past seven in the evening, shop at gas station convenience stores, or use skateboards on any public property."

Blue Eyes raised their brows, frowned, opened their mouths, and swallowed their words. Brody Brinkman rolled his very pale blue eyes and crossed his arms; Jessica Dobie bent to tie her shoe, muttering something about *insane.*

Mr. Hudson addressed the Seated Ones. "How do you feel about the Commission's announcement?"

"Why only kids with blue eyes?" asked Annette Stuckey. "That doesn't make sense."

"Yeah, like Brody is some gangster," said Justin Thayer. "You go, Bro."

Complaints flew: "Not fair." "Rip-off." "It stinks."

"This isn't for real, is it, Mr. H?" said Noelle Laslett.

My chest tightened and my skin tingled hot. But I should be okay. I had brown eyes.

"Blue Eyes, you may sit down." Mr. Hudson kept his serious voice.

Another round of restless chairs and grumbles.

"Okay. How do you feel, Blue Eyes?" Mr. Hudson went to the whiteboard.

"Are we allowed to talk now?" Peter Monroe shot back.

"Be my guest," said Mr. Hudson, marker in hand.

"You can't make someone do this stuff just 'cause they have blue eyes. It's totally ridiculous. Who is this experimental Commission, anyway? What are they trying to do?"

Mr. Hudson wrote *confused* on the board.

"Yeah, a lot more than *confused*," said Peter, his voice rising, "but I can't say it in school except it starts with a *p* and rhymes with *missed*."

We choked back uneasy laughs as Mr. Hudson wrote *missed*. "More feelings," he said.

Annette raised her hand. "It's scary. Kids won't do it and there'll be fights and people getting hurt."

Scared went on the board. "Maybe there will be policemen watching," said Mr. Hudson, "guarding, checking IDs, arresting disobedient Blue Eyes."

"No way!" Justin practically jumped out of his seat.

"Come on, Mr. H, what's going on? This kind of thing doesn't happen here in Oregon, in the United States of America."

Mr. Hudson wrote *disbelief* and *trusting*. "I appreciate your heartfelt responses. To reassure those who didn't listen carefully, this is an *experiment* in this classroom — not in Yamhill County." He walked over to his desk and picked up a book. "This, however, was *not* a fictitious experiment." He turned a few pages, then began reading:

> After May 1940 good times rapidly fled: first the war, then the capitulation, followed by the arrival of the Germans, which is when the sufferings of us Jews really began. Anti-Jewish decrees followed each other in quick succession. Jews must wear a yellow star, Jews must hand in their bicycles, Jews are banned from trams and are forbidden to drive. Jews are only allowed to do their shopping between three and five o'clock and then only in shops which bear the placard 'Jewish shop.' Jews must be indoors by eight o'clock and cannot even sit in their own gardens after that hour. Jews are forbidden to visit theaters, cinemas, and other places of entertainment. Jews may not take part in public sports. Swimming baths,

tennis courts, hockey fields, and other sports grounds are all prohibited to them. Jews may not visit Christians. Jews must go to Jewish schools. . . .

Mr. Hudson closed the book and looked out the window as if the red and yellow maple leaves could tell him what to say next. When he returned to the room, to us, it was with the heavy face of someone about to deliver bad news. He held up the book so we could see the cover. A black-and-white photograph showed a girl with dark hair, deep-set eyes (were they blue?), and a sweet smile looking at our class. *Anne Frank: The Diary of a Young Girl.*

"This is the famous diary of a girl just about your age, who lived in hiding for two years, fearful of discovery by the German Nazis, who moved past rules and restrictions to removing Jews from their homes, placing them in ghettos, slave-labor camps, and death camps."

Mr. Hudson's voice had softened until he practically whispered *death camps.* "To begin our unit on European history, we are going to study the Holocaust, a very serious time in world history when human beings did horrific, inhumane things. No, there isn't a County Commission on Youth Safety, but maybe there's something less obvious lurking out there. More than anything, I want you to watch for prejudices in our lives today, compare them to events of the Holocaust, and observe how unspoken attitudes grow into a loud, collective voice."

He looked at us for a moment, letting the words sink in. "You are excused, now, to the library to get your own copy of Anne Frank's diary. Please study all the introductory photos and read to September 29, 1942, by Monday."

After checking out my book, I headed for Noelle and Jessica, but my steps slowed as I glanced at the cover, at Anne Frank's bright, unsuspecting eyes. *May not. Must. Only. Banned.* Mr. Hudson's words echoed in my ears. *Forbidden. Lived in hiding. Suffering.* My heart pounded faster, louder. Surely everyone could hear. I took a deep breath. It wasn't enough. Another breath and my legs and arms went limp. *I told you. You never listen.* A different voice now. *You're a pathetic loser.* My head spun in confusion. *Hopeless.* A woman's voice. *Helpless. Clueless.* My mother's voice! But why now? In the school library? And why did the sound of her voice make me sick? Could eleven-year-olds have heart attacks? Was I going crazy? I moved in slow motion, praying for an empty seat.

A red blob loomed before me, and with steady urging, my rubber legs shuffled three, four more steps. Then I dropped into a soft, squishy nest, which swallowed my shaking body. I sat there, eyes closed, head spinning, the drumbeats in my ears slowly fading and my body sighing. Something nudged my arm and I cracked one eye open, expecting to see, of all people, my mother standing there, pointing her finger at me, telling me to *shape up or ship out.*

Instead, it was the half-free body of a mashed teddy bear. I rocked to one side, pulled him out, and allowed my arms to wrap around his fat chest, my head melting into his fuzzy, thick neck.

I'd made my way to the kiddie corner, empty and

quiet. Something hard jabbed my other side. Now what? I pulled out a picture book with pale blue stars and a big full moon, orange dancing flames in a black fire-place, and a cow jumping through the night sky. *Goodnight Moon,* sang the bright yellow letters. "In the great green room," I whispered to Bear, pulling him closer; turning the pages; floating on words about mit-tens and kittens, clocks and socks; stirring my first *Goodnight Moon* memory: Annette's sixth birthday and my first slumber party. I was so excited to be invited, to play games, eat cake, and sleep on the floor. But the best part was the bedtime story. Annette's mother sat on the sofa with Annette on her lap. A couple kids were cross-legged on the floor, one girl was on the sofa next to Annette's mom, and I was on the other side.

"Let's snuggle," said Mrs. Stuckey, hugging Annette. I inched closer and felt her mother's warm body next to mine. She began reading *Goodnight Moon* in a sparkly voice, stopping to show us the pictures and letting us find the mouse. She leaned forward and put her finger on her lips to whisper "hush." Then she slipped her arm around my shoulder, letting Annette turn the pages. An Angel Mom.

"Mr. Hudson's class — return to your room, please," came our librarian's voice. Kids jumped up, chairs slammed against tables. "Quietly." I gave Bear a tight hug, left *Goodnight Moon* on his lap, and walked back to class, relieved that my heart had slowed down and my legs had sped up.

That night I sat in bed, my lamp sending shadows around the room. I stared at the words I'd just read in Anne Frank's diary; honest, regretful words about her friends only having fun and joking, like they were stuck in one spot and could never get closer.

I thought of Noelle and Jessica and our conversations about school and teachers, music and movies. But what about deep, serious thoughts? I should have some by now. Shouldn't I? My only thoughts were getting through each day and staying out of trouble. *And* going to Outdoor School! That was enough. For now.

I crawled out of bed to the jumble of stuffed animals in the corner by my closet and chose my yellow and green turtle. She joined me back in bed, sitting on my lap, gazing at my bedroom walls — a dough map of Oregon with half of Mount Hood broken off, my Jefferson County mural from fourth grade, a poster of a sunflower, and my first-grade star chart. The shiny stars — for keeping my school desk clean, remembering my homework, walking in line to the cafeteria, and being a good listener at circle time — marched across the paper.

When Mrs. Atkins gave me my chart at the end of the year, she said, "Good job, Hope. Keep it up." I suppose she meant keep up the good work, but maybe she meant keep the chart up on my wall. I don't know for sure, but I do know it still makes me proud to see all those silver and gold and purple stars.

"Goodnight, stars," I said, smiling at the silliness. "Goodnight, map. Goodnight, Turtle, on my lap." Ha! Not bad. I closed my book and turned out my light. "Goodnight, Anne," I whispered, respecting the silence of her hiding.

CHAPTER 4

Stupid

The next day was Mom's birthday. I told her "happy birthday" at breakfast and gave her a card I'd made with gold glitter and pink sequins.

"That's very sweet, Hope. Thank you, darling." She smiled, planted a kiss on my cheek, and put the card on the fridge with a heavy-duty magnet and a sigh.

"Happy over the hill," said Tyler, dropping bread into the toaster.

Mom eyed him. "Not funny." She sat down at the table with another, louder sigh.

I poured a bowl of cereal and whispered to Tyler, "What's *over the hill*?"

"You're anciently old," he whispered back. "It's all

downhill, one foot in the grave." His toast popped up. "It's a joke." Then he raised his voice. "But not everyone can take a joke."

Mom ignored him. She pulled something out of her bathrobe pocket and flicked a lighter. A cigarette! I'd never seen my mother smoke. Maybe it was a fortieth-birthday thing. *Over the hill* with a cigarette. I stood there staring as she sat there smoking and looking out the window.

So I ate my cereal, Tyler ate his toast, and we exchanged glances while Mom smoked *another* cigarette. I guess I couldn't blame her if she wasn't feeling so hot. I mean, 40 isn't exactly a great number. The 4 looks like it can't decide which way it wants to go and the 0 is that circle business again.

I put the Wheaties and the jug of milk away, made my bed, brushed my teeth, and was heading for the bus —

"Hope Marie Elliot! COME HERE RIGHT NOW!"

I froze. My heart sank. My brain raced for a defense, but what was there to defend? Mom always liked the beginning of a new school year. Back to a routine, she said every September. And I'd been role modeling like crazy, smiling and saying hi to the fifth graders, keeping my room picked up and my radio turned down. There'd even been good numbers: 6:42 when I went to the bathroom (I *love* even numbers!), 10:10 at bedtime. Things had been good, and I'd wished for the zillionth time that they'd stay that way. Forever.

"HOPE MAAARIEEE!"

My pounding heart reminded me once again of the rhythm of my life. Good, then bad. High, then low. Cautious, then careless. As I returned to the kitchen, my entire body hit high alert, braced for the changing tide. The tidal wave.

Mom leaned against the sink, arms crossed, jaw clenched, eyes locked on mine, eyebrows raised, aimed, ready to fire.

"What do you see on the table?"

Warning. Trick question. Warning. Mind to mouth: Take your time. Get it right. Be sure. "Place mats . . . newspaper . . . jam . . . salt and pepper . . ."

"Don't be smart with me, young lady." Her finger stabbed the air in time with the sharp words. "You are so damn stupid. You know exactly what I'm talking about."

My mind whirled faster and faster like one of those carnival rides, spinning, twisting, turning upside down. I held my breath. Heat throbbed up my face and down my neck. If I knew exactly what she was talking about, why didn't I know the answer?

Maybe I should just give up, surrender. *Mind to eyes: sad, sorry, will never do it again.* I stared at the white puddle resting undisturbed in the bottom of my cereal bowl. What would it be like to float in a pool of silky, cool milk, gazing up at —

"You dumb shit! I am not the goddamned maid!" Mom snatched the bowl, milk slopping over the rim and down her bathrobe. "I have picked up after you for eleven lousy years. I'm sick and tired of it. You don't appreciate a single thing I do. You never listen. Get out! Get outta my sight! GET!"

Think Happy Thoughts. That's hard to do when you're sitting in the principal's office, but that's what the framed sign said, stitched in red and blue *X*s.

I wondered if principals had happy thoughts. At least Mrs. Piersma had a happy office: flowery wallpaper, a flowery bulletin board, flowery curtains, plus real flowers in a green vase. I spotted the clear glass bowl on the corner of her desk filled with red-and-white striped peppermint candies. One of those would give me happy thoughts.

I took a deep breath and sat back in the soft chair. With the door closed, I could barely hear office voices — probably Mrs. Piersma telling the secretary my mom would be coming soon.

I shuddered. Of all days. I'd already made her mad. Forgetting my cereal bowl! How stupid was that? How could I have missed it? Probably laughing at one of Tyler's jokes. Now she had to come to the principal's office and do her acting thing. Thank goodness she had the day off and was going out to lunch with her old high school friend, Lydia Bishop. Or, maybe that wasn't such a good thing. I didn't know anymore.

Now the principal's door opened and Mrs. Piersma walked in. She closed the door and smiled. Her red lipstick matched her earrings. "It's good to see you, Hope. How are you doing?"

I shrugged and looked down at the carpet (no flowers).

"Am I kicked off the bus?"

Mrs. Piersma pulled a chair next to mine and sat down as if we were going to have a friendly little chat. She smiled again, like a grandmother smiles at her grandbaby.

"You know, Hope, about our zero-tolerance bus behavior?"

I nodded. But did she have to call Mom?

"I'm afraid you're not going to be able to ride for a week. Can your mother bring you to school?"

I cringed, knowing Mom's reaction: "Hope is such an inconvenience," like I was some 7-Eleven store that had closed at ten.

"So," said Mrs. Piersma, trying to sound all cheery, "how does it feel to be a sixth grader?"

"Okay," I muttered.

"And you have Outdoor School next spring. I bet you're looking forward to that."

I nodded. Yeah. Terrific. I'm probably already on the *Bad Role Model, One-More-Mistake-And-You're-Not-Going* list. My gut twisted.

I heard Mom's voice as she talked to the secretary. I gripped the chair. The door whipped open and Mom's eyes nailed mine.

My head jerked back.

Mrs. Piersma stood up and offered her a seat, but Mom didn't move, her fists mashed into her hips. "Hope is so damn irresponsible. What did the little brat do *this* time?"

"Ms. Elliot," said Mrs. Piersma, lowering her voice, "I understand you're upset, but could you please refrain from swearing in the school?" Mrs. Piersma stood taller and straighter, like she was guarding Eola Hills Grade School.

I sat there, mouth open, eyeballs jumping back and forth, waiting for a fight.

Mom suddenly smiled sweetly, sat down, and folded her hands in her lap. "Excuse me, Mrs. Piersma," she said very businesslike. "It's my birthday today and I've got a lot on my mind. Could you please tell me again why Hope is in trouble?" She gave me a fake smile. "Can't Hope cope?"

Breakfast threatened my throat.

Mrs. Piersma spoke carefully. "I'm sure Hope didn't mean what she said on the bus. She has apologized to the girl and she'll be doing some cleanup work around the school. But she won't be able to ride the bus for a week."

"What in the world did you say, Hope?" I felt my mother's hot glare as I stared at *Think Happy Thoughts*. I tried thinking bad thoughts, about something happening to Mom, but it didn't make me feel better, just sad. I mean, there were some good times.

"Hope Marie." There. Just like that. A gentle voice, a soft hint of care. A happy flash. I longed to stay with my mother in that very moment, in Mrs. Piersma's office, forever.

I closed my eyes. "I called Danielle Moffat a 'dumb shit.'"

"Oh." It came out a relieved *oh*. My eyes opened.

"An accident," she said, turning to Mrs. Piersma. "I'm so sorry. I'm sure it won't happen again. Hope will be punished at home, but could she still ride the bus? It would be extremely inconvenient for me to drive her to school."

"I'm sorry, Mrs. Elliot, but this is school policy."

Mom's face turned as hard as those presidents' faces carved in cliffs. She stood up. "Then Hope will just have to walk."

CHAPTER 5

Life Is Crazy

I was a mess the rest of the day. I was so tired I just stared at the whiteboard, or at Mr. Hudson's bald spot, or at the windy showers of dried-up maple leaves. What a relief when Mr. Hudson pulled down the blinds and centered the TV/VCR in front of the room. Good, I could go to sleep.

Mr. Hudson held up the video cover. *Life Is Beautiful*, it said on it, with a man, lady, and little boy, all laughing and smiling. "This is the story of a Jewish father's daring imagination and quick thinking to protect his young son from racism and save him from the Nazi gas chambers."

He slipped the movie into the player. "How many of you have seen a foreign film?"

Silence.

"Okay. This is how it works. The actors will be speaking in Italian, but their words will appear in English at the bottom of the screen."

"Like you were deaf?" asked Katie Shelton.

Mr. Hudson nodded. "Yes, Katie, like closed-captioned TV."

"So we have to read?" Justin Thayer winced. "*While* we're watching the movie?"

"*And* write," said Mr. Hudson. "In the first part of the movie look for two signs of racism, and in the second part look for three survival strategies."

Darn. So much for my nap.

"Survival strategies?" Justin asked again.

"You know what a strategy is, don't you?" said Mr. Hudson.

"Like in basketball," said Brody. "We have offense and defense strategies."

"Right," said Mr. Hudson. "A plan. A means to reach your goal. And survival?"

"How you're going to live through something," said Brody.

"Right, again."

"Yeah, like surviving this assignment," said Justin.

We laughed.

"There are some funny moments in this story," said Mr. Hudson, "but humor is meant to open your heart so you can see beyond the moment to the bigger picture: the craziness, the sadness, and the tragedy."

I had my paper on my desk and pencil in hand, ready to find the answers, but both were soon forgotten as I fell into a rhythm, listening to the Italian dialogue, reading the English subtitles, and trying to keep up with this guy named Guido who's always cracking jokes and doing wild things to make people smile or laugh.

One time he pokes fun at the Race Manifesto, which declares non-Jewish Italians are of a superior race. Before you know it, Guido is taking off his clothes, down to his underwear, and he pulls up his T-shirt, saying that Italians have great belly buttons.

Funny Guido marries sweet Dora and they have a little boy, Joshua. It seems the perfect life in this small Italian town, with sunny days and flowers and Guido always teasing and laughing with Dora and Joshua.

But I found my stomach tightening, sensing things were about to change. Just like for Anne Frank.

The little signs, like Mr. Hudson said, began showing up. Like the Nazi soldiers, marching down the streets. And a poster in the bakery: "No Jews or dogs allowed."

All of a sudden, Guido and Joshua are forced onto a Nazi army truck and hauled off to a train station. Guido tells his son they're going on a trip for Joshua's birthday, and they're so lucky because they got the last tickets for the train and they *get* to stand real close together because trains don't have seats.

But I knew different. I knew by now those trains led to a nightmare — the German concentration camps. I sat there in my safe classroom, so worried for Joshua, who had no idea that people hated him and wanted to kill him just because he was Jewish. *Get off the train! I desperately wanted to warn them. Run! Hide! Before it's too late!*

Then, out of nowhere, comes Dora, all dressed up for Joshua's birthday in this red suit and hat and high heels, telling the guard that she has to get on the train with her husband and son. The guard checks the list and says her name isn't on it (she's not Jewish). But she won't give up. She demands to get on the train. They finally let her climb into one of the packed boxcars. Joshua sees her through the metal grille of a nearby car and cries out, "They stopped the train to let Mama get on!"

When they reach the Nazi concentration camp, Guido tells Joshua they're playing a game and if they win, they get first prize. "What is it?" asks Joshua. Guido names Joshua's favorite toy, an army tank. "But I already have one," Joshua replies.

"A real one," Guido quickly responds, and explains the rules. They must accumulate one thousand points by not asking for a snack or wanting to see Mommy, or crying to go home. A plain piece of bread with no jam is worth sixty points.

"Is sixty points a lot?" asks Joshua. "It sure is," says his father. "And if you stay hidden all day it's a hundred and twenty points."

Every time I feared for Joshua's life, his father came up with a clever plan. Every time Joshua questioned the game or repeated horrible rumors, Guido zipped out a perfect answer or awarded more points.

Thank you, I thought, wishing Guido could hear me. *You are an amazing father.*

At the end of the movie, the United States Army is coming and the Germans are madly pushing Jewish prisoners into trucks, hoping to get rid of a few more loads. Guido is frantic. He quickly hides Joshua, urging him not to come out of the small cupboard, telling him they've earned a thousand points and they've won the grand prize, the tank. Then he's off again, disguised as a woman, racing to find Dora, madly searching, calling, then shouting at her to escape from the departing truck. As he's warning her, he is discovered and captured. A Nazi soldier marches him to a nearby alley. They disappear into darkness.

A gun fires.

Oh, no! Tears filled my eyes and fell to my blank paper.

The concentration camp is deserted. Quiet. Fires burning. Hidden prisoners begin appearing and Joshua comes out of his cupboard. All of a sudden, a U.S. tank comes around the corner and Joshua's eyes grow huge. "It's true!" he says. The tank stops right in front of him and out pops an army guy speaking English. "Want a ride?" he asks Joshua.

Everyone in the classroom started clapping. My throat tightened and my eyes blurred.

As the tank follows the road lined with departing prisoners, Joshua spots his mother in the crowd. "Mama!" he cries, and the soldier lowers him into his mother's arms. They sit alongside the road, hugging and kissing. "We won!" Joshua announces. "We came in first!" Then a man's voice tells us: "This is my story. This is the sacrifice my father made. This was his gift to me."

I shivered and realized Mr. Hudson had turned off the TV. The room was still dark but I could see him leaning against the TV cart, his head bent. My nose dripped but I didn't move to wipe it. Someone sniffled, sighed. A cough.

"I'm sorry." Mr. Hudson gently touched the silence. "I didn't plan this very well." He glanced at the clock. "The bell is about to ring and something this serious deserves more time. You'll probably feel a little strange going home with kids who have no clue what you just went through. Stay focused, if you can; try to remember what you saw; let it sink in; think about the questions; talk with your parents, as they allowed you to see this film."

The bell rang but no one moved.

Slowly, one by one, kids began shuffling their chairs and standing up.

Someone turned on the lights. I squinted and met Noelle's watery eyes. Justin walked to the door staring at the floor. I didn't want to go home; I wanted to rewind the film and stop at a happy spot, before all the hurting and pain.

CHAPTER 6

Next to New

Why did it always rain when I had to walk home? I trudged away from school, hoping Anne Frank wouldn't get wet in my backpack. Not that I had miles to go, but it was a good fifteen- to twenty-minute fast walk. I wasn't in any fast mood, though. Not after that movie. I kept thinking about Joshua and his mother and what I'd give for that kind of reunion. I could still hear his excited voice: "MAMA!" Maybe my mother would miss me if I was lost in the woods or held hostage in a bank robbery. "HOPE!" she'd shout as I raced into her arms.

I'd just passed Eola Hills Pizza and Coastal Bank, staying dry beneath their awnings, when I saw the boots.

They were purple. Well, mostly purple, with some brown and green designs. The bottoms were thick black rubber. There I stood, nose pressed to the window, my breath washing the cold glass, my heart craving those beautiful boots.

I barely noticed the yellow ski jacket and red backpack in the Next to New display. Actually, I'd barely noticed the store before. Mom said she'd never set foot in one of those musty-smelling consignment shops, let alone in someone else's shoes. But these boots looked brand-new and I could just see myself in them at Outdoor School.

A bell jangled as I opened the door. I braced myself for knockdown body odor and an instant skin rash, but nothing happened.

The woman behind the cash register smiled.

"Could I try on the purple hiking boots?" I pointed to the window display.

I sat on a bench and slipped off my tennis shoes.

The woman handed me the boots. Her name tag said "*Anita* — Owner/Manager." I quickly put them on, winding the leather laces around the top hooks and tying a thick bow. Oh, man, did they feel great. I stood and looked at Anita. She pushed her glasses into her orangish hair, examined my feet, and announced, "Awesome."

They were heavier than I'd expected, but they made my feet feel strong. Same with my legs. I could march across the country, or at least across Oregon. For now, I walked around the store, weaving in and out of dresses, pants, jackets, baby clothes, and wedding gowns. I stole glances into the full-length mirrors, trying not to smile at cool me, taller me.

I bent over to check the price and wished I hadn't: $14. All I had was $5.45 sitting in a glass jar in my top dresser drawer.

I hiked over to Anita, now laughing and sorting through a pile of clothes with another name-tagged lady: *Ruthie* — Asst. Manager."

"How do you pay for things here?" I asked. "I mean, can I put these on layaway?"

Ruthie inspected my feet. "You can pay for those

gorgeous boots by letting us sell your nice, outgrown clothes." She handed me a flyer: *Welcome. We're pleased you want to be part of our clothing family. Here's how it works.*

I was to wash and iron my clothes, place them on hangers, and bring them to the store. I'd receive forty percent of the selling price. My mind shot through my closet and drawers. Jeans, too small. T-shirt with teddy bears and valentines, too babyish. There was a lot of stuff crammed in the back of my drawers and under my bed.

"To hold the boots," said Anita, as if we were about to close a big business deal, "you'd need to give us twenty percent of the price. That would be two dollars and eighty cents."

"No problem. I've got that at home. I'll bring it right back. Please don't sell them while I'm gone."

As I tugged the boots off, she added, "The rest needs to be paid in two weeks."

Two weeks!

"Otherwise," she added, "you lose your down payment."

"How soon will my clothes sell?"

She shrugged. "You never know, but bring in winter clothes now and save your spring and summer things for later."

I jogged most of the way home, jumping puddles, imagining myself in those amazing boots at Outdoor School, leading the trek up Lava Butte.

I stopped at an intersection to catch my breath. Leaning against the streetlight, I felt my heart throbbing in my neck. It was a good throbbing, though, not a bad throbbing like in Mrs. Piersma's office that morning. But she'd been extra nice after Mom had left. "Are you okay?" she'd asked, handing me two pieces of candy.

"Yeah," I'd said, stuffing them in my pants pocket. *I could live here in your office, eat peppermint candies, and have happy thoughts. I'd never have to ride the bus again and I'd always be on time.*

"Come visit me again, Hope," said Mrs. Piersma, "just for fun."

Since when did you visit the principal *just for fun*? And why did she sound more sad than happy?

The sky had turned dark now with another rain cloud. Car headlights glowed in the road spray. I shivered and started jogging again. Better get home before Mom. Not that I was doing anything wrong, but there were always questions and she definitely wouldn't like the Next to New business. I'd have to hear all the reasons why I shouldn't even open their door.

My heart sank as I turned up our driveway and saw Mom's car in the garage. I fumbled in my pocket for a peppermint.

"Where have you been?" Mom stood in front of the open refrigerator, her back to me.

"I had to walk, *remember*?" I knew it was smarty to remind her, but I couldn't help it. My feet were freezing.

She jerked around, a plastic bottle of mustard in her hand, the nozzle pointed at me. I could imagine mustard splattering all over me and the kitchen and I couldn't help smiling.

"Wipe that nasty smirk off your face right this instant." She shook the bottle at me. "Your punishment *was* to stay in your room tomorrow. Now it's the *whole* weekend, starting right this minute!"

"But I wasn't smirking. It was just funny seeing you shake the mustard bottle."

"You dumb shit! Don't you dare talk back to me!"

"I'm not."

"Don't argue."

"I'm not. Can't I come out at all?"

"You can go to the bathroom and eat in the kitchen. That's it."

"What about the laundry room? I gotta wash my clothes."

"So wash them."

"And dry."

"FINE."

"Iron?"

"SHUT your stupid mouth UP!" She slammed the mustard on the table. "God, girl, you really know how to push. Get out of here — right now."

My boots! I had to tell Anita I wasn't coming back. "Just one phone call."

"No calls."

I went to my room and fell onto my bed, my cold bare feet sticky against the comforter. *Shut up! Shut up! Shut up!* I said the words out loud, face crammed into my pillow, but my entire body ached to scream them as loud as my voice could carry them; right out my door, down the hall, into my mother's face. Why not? She said them to me.

CHAPTER 7

A Secret Place

I stood at my bedroom window and stared into the black night. Rain splattered against the glass and cold air slipped past the rattling wood frame. Maybe I should just open the window, slip out, and find a new life. It was an exciting thought, a huge relief, but one that should have a plan. Besides, I'd had enough wet feet for a while and I did have plans — not big ones like running away, but busy ones to keep my mind off Mom and the purple boots.

Plan A: Change into Dry Clothes. Sweats and slippers.

Plan B: Clothes for Next to New. I opened my dresser drawers one by one, took everything out, and laid them on my bed according to: 1) Save for me 2) Sell at Next to New 3) Give to Goodwill. Underwear, T-shirts, jeans, shorts, socks. Some of the stuff, like my rainbow pajamas, I hadn't worn in years.

I did the same thing with my closet clothes, getting rid of little-girl dresses, short skirts, blouses that untucked, wornout belts, and outgrown shoes. One final place: under my bed. Ugh. Scrunched clothes smothered in dust bunnies.

I like our laundry room. It's small and tidy — shelves for soap and bleach; baskets for ironing, mending, and rags; drawers with sewing supplies and wrapping paper. When I close the door and turn on the ceiling fan, I feel like I'm in charge: full load, one scoop soap, hot wash, cold rinse, extra spin. Check, check, check. All systems go.

I pushed *Start*. Water rushed against the metal tub. The laundry room echoed with a chorus of hum, drum, whirl.

Now I was in a cleaning mood. Without being told, I gathered rags, paper towels, Endust, and Windex, and headed back to my bedroom prison. Starting with my dresser, I went around the room spraying and wiping furniture, windows, and the mirrors on my closet sliding door. I even dusted my stuffed animals.

Plan C: My Closet. All this digging out and cleaning up made me think of Anne Frank and her family settling into their hidden "Secret Annexe," with the unpacking of boxes, sewing and hanging of curtains, scrubbing of floors, and decorating of walls, all to make it feel safe and normal.

With my next trip to the laundry room, I brought back extra blankets, a pillow and pillowcase. I stretched my bedside lamp into the closet and arranged the bedding in there. I lined all my stuffed animals along the back. Then I taped a newspaper picture of Gabriela Feliciano to the wall. Turtle sat on top of my pillow, and Anne Frank's diary lay on the blanket.

"Dinner's ready." Mom's voice approached. I jumped out of the closet and shut the door just in time. The bedroom door swung open and she examined the piles on my bed.

"I — I decided to wash everything," I said, avoiding her eyes.

"That'll keep you busy this weekend. You can do mine when you're done." She laughed like it was a joke. "Seriously, Hope, your room looks great."

My eyes shot to hers. Yes, they *were* smiling, along with her mouth. Wow. My face heated and I tried not to smile back, but I couldn't help it. Now maybe she'd visit every day and tell me — in a light, sunny voice — "Hope, your room looks great. You look great. You have great ears and a great nose and eyebrows and —"

"Wash your hands. They're filthy."

We sat across the table from each other, eating spaghetti. Flowers and a funny birthday card decorated Tyler's place. He'd given them to Mom, wished her happy birthday, then left for Egan McGowan's for the night. Smart guy.

Mom looked relaxed in her baggy Detroit Lions sweatshirt and flannel pj bottoms, no earrings, hair pulled back into a ponytail, makeup washed off.

She let out a huge sigh. "I can't tell you how stressed I am."

I concentrated on twirling noodles around my fork.

"I race off to work, put in a long day, stop by the grocery store, fix dinner, harp on you two to do homework, iron my clothes for the next day." She took a bite and I wondered if we'd ever have a different conversation.

"Are you listening to me, Hope Marie? Have you heard a single word I've said? Look at me when I'm talking to you."

I looked.

"Repeat my last sentence."

I hate the listening test. It always comes when you're not listening. "Look at me when I'm talking to you," I said, immediately regretting the wrong answer.

Mom's mouth tightened and I imagined a rattlesnake's tongue flicking out of her mouth, ready to strike. She dropped her fork into her spaghetti, crossed her arms on the table, and glared.

I felt the prick of tears but fought them back. As a little girl, I'd cried at my mother's angry face and stabbing words, but over the years I've tried to block them from my ears and from my gut, where they turned to inside tears. It doesn't always work, though. I just wished I understood how she could be so nice one minute and so angry the next — like she was two different people.

"My advice to you, young lady," Mom said, with her fork pointing at me, "don't get married and don't have kids."

With that bit of wisdom stuck in my brain and French bread stuck in my teeth, I returned to the laundry room. I plodded through another wash/dry cycle, folded clothes that were staying, sacked Goodwill stuff, and hung out clothes to iron. When I crawled into my closet that night, I was exhausted, but not so wiped out as to miss the sweet peacefulness drifting down . . . floating across my bed, my pillow, Turtle, and me. There, in my narrow, dark closet, with the sliding door barely opened, I felt strangely safe and happy. I hugged Turtle, settled into my pillow, and thought about my purple hiking boots. I could see the heavy, thick soles; I could smell the outdoors; and I crossed my fingers they'd still be there Monday.

CHAPTER 8

Number the Stars

The next morning I awoke still holding Turtle, neither one of us having moved an inch all night. I looked straight up, into the uneven shadows of dresses, skirts, blouses, and pants. After all that sorting, washing, and cleaning business yesterday, these leftover clothes seemed like old friends.

Mom was still asleep and Tyler was still at Egan's. I like having breakfast by myself. I can fix whatever I want without anyone eyeing my every move, telling me I shouldn't cook the eggs so long or that I should toast the bread longer. That morning I made fluffy scrambled eggs, golden brown toast, and a pitcher of orange juice. When I was done eating, I cleared the table, put everything away, loaded my dishes in the dishwasher, and wiped sticky juice drops off the floor. Surely Mom would notice how clean I'd left things and then she'd drop the rest of my punishment.

I started another load of laundry and was folding clothes when Mom opened my bedroom door. "Don't ever take the last eggs. Someone else might want them, too, you know." I started to tell her about cleaning up, but she slammed the door. I opened it after her. "Can I iron in front of the TV?"

"No."

"Why not?"

She spun around. BIG SIGH. "Today is Saturday. I've worked hard all week and I need at least one day of peace and quiet. So don't bug me or I'll make it two weekends."

I closed the door, leaned against it, and inspected my room — the walls, the window, my swivel chair, desk, and star chart. Five hundred stars. That's what this punishment should be worth. I closed my eyes and imagined myself flying like a bird, free to go wherever I wanted, high above snowy mountains or skimming low across the ocean to a tropical island with palm trees and pineapples. Or into a sparkling night sky, dancing from star to star, making my own pattern: the Hope Constellation.

Suddenly I saw Joshua in the concentration camp, stamping his foot and telling his father he wanted to go home. "They're mean here. They yell." I'll bet his father wished he could have flown Joshua away, but instead he created the clever point system for distraction, for the real army tank.

Problem Solve: I needed a distraction. And a prize. I deserved a prize for all the hours in this room. A prize for my mother's sighing and glaring, for "stupid," "brat," and "dumb shit."

That's when it hit — a great idea, a great distraction. I hurried to my desk and looked through the drawers, finding a little spiral notebook with a black Lab puppy on the front. On the first page I wrote "HOPE'S POINT SYSTEM." After lots of writing, crossing out, erasing, and rewriting, this is what came out:

FB = Feel Bad	20–150 Points
G = Grab	25 Points
SA = Sarcasm	35 Points
GL = Glare	40 Points
LO = Loser	50 Points
SH = Should	60 Points
HL = Hopeless	75 Points
LA = Laughed At	75 Points
B = Brat	85 Points
DS = Dumb Shit	100 Points
I = Interrupt	100 Points
SW = Swear Word	150 Points
S = Stupid	200 Points

Now I needed a prize, but not an army tank. I'd have to think about it.

Any thoughts about prizes disappeared the rest of the day as I read *Anne Frank: The Diary of a Young Girl.* I couldn't believe my eyes when I read the mean things people in hiding said to her. Check this out: "Am I really so bad-mannered, conceited, headstrong, pushing, stupid, lazy, etc., etc., as they all say? . . . Kitty, if only you knew how I sometimes boil under so many gibes and jeers. And I don't know how long I shall be able to stifle my rage. I shall just blow up one day."

It felt strange that someone so long ago could have had the same feelings I had. Anne needed a point system like Joshua's and mine. Instead, she had her best friend, Kitty, her diary to talk to. I named my notebook Penny. Have you heard people say, "A penny for your thoughts?"

CHAPTER 9

Plans into Action

By Sunday afternoon I thought my arm was going to fall off, but I wasn't done yet. I still wanted to wash and iron all the clothes I planned to keep. I'd discovered clothes I hadn't worn for a long time but still fit me, like a white blouse with glittery stars on the pocket and a pair of black jeans I didn't like before, but now I do. It was fun to think about wearing something different for a change.

I poked into the living room where Mom and Tyler were watching a football game. "Do you guys have any extra hangers?"

"In my closet," said Mom, her eyes glued to the TV.

"You can iron my stuff." Tyler tossed me his spongy football.

I threw it back, hitting his head, and stuck out my tongue. "Forget it."

"Careful, Missy," said Mom.

"Of what?" As soon as I'd said it, I knew I'd gone too far. WHY did I do that??? WHY did I push???

"Hope Marie." Firm but not a raised voice. Whew. Just a warning. But she GLARED. Yes! My first 40 points!

"I'm going." I practically skipped down the hall to her room, grinning like I'd just won a contest.

When I reached her bedroom door, I wasn't so excited. In fact, this was pretty stupid. Why would I want to win an arguing contest with my mom? It always made things worse. Yet, there was something itching inside me, scratching to get out, to stir her up, and I let it happen.

Problem Solve: Points for Not Talking Back. NTB: 50 Points. Just think, if I'd bitten my tongue on the bus, I wouldn't be a weekend prisoner.

Mom's closet door stood open like someone's mouth showing off a mishmash of partly chewed food. Mixed-up shoes spilled into the room; dresses hung lopsided; her bathrobe, nightgown, and last week's pants overloaded the door hook; and a mountain of dirty clothes guarded the closet floor.

I pawed through the jam-packed rack, collecting a handful of empty hangers. As I reached the end, something sparked a memory. I pulled out the last hanger and stared at the dress. Then I walked over to Mom's dresser. There she was, in that silver-framed photo, wearing the same blue-and-white-checkered sundress. Holding me. Brand New Me wrapped in a baby blanket. Just home from the hospital, she'd told me. She was smiling. Not a pretend actress smile. She looked like she was really happy to have me.

I dropped the empty hangers on the floor and slowly sat down on her unmade bed. Still hugging the checkered dress, I snuggled under her sheet and blanket, nestling my head in her pillow, smelling her hair. I closed my eyes and tried to imagine my mother walking up to our house with me in her arms and Tyler running outside begging to see me, hold me. My throat tightened. Should I get points for not crying?

It was almost dinner and I was finally done. Everything was washed, ironed, hung up, or folded in dresser drawers.

I turned slowly in my swivel chair, surveying my room. The furniture glowed and the mirrors shined. But, now, without anything to do, I heard the silence. It moved slowly around my room, slipped along the walls, brushed across my arms, filled my ears, and gnawed my gut. Was this how it felt in prison? Was this how Anne Frank felt all those whispering, tiptoeing days in the "Secret Annexe"? It was a lonely silence shouting all the things you couldn't do, places you couldn't go.

Well, there's one thing you end up doing with a lot of silence — you think. You think about how life could be better and you make up little plans like getting a dog or cat to keep you company or having a best friend that tells you all her secrets. You put together big plans like running away, listing in your head the clothes you'll need, the kinds of food that won't smash or spoil, the backstreet route to the bus station; buying a ticket to Portland and heading up Highway 99W through Newberg and Tigard; finding the runaway shelter.

But what about Tyler? I'd miss Tyler, even though I didn't see much of him now that he was in high school. But he still opened my door and threw things at me; made me laugh with some funny story, imitating the teachers or lip-synching country-western singers. It's always been Tyler who's gotten me through the rough times with Mom. He's come to my rescue, teasing Mom out of her bad moods. Why she's nice to him, I don't know. Maybe she just likes boys better. Maybe he wasn't an accident.

Someone knocked on my door. "HeyHop! Let's go! Dinner!" Speaking of my brother.

I jumped up and whipped open my door.

"Out of my way!" I pushed him down the hall and stepped on his feet. He grabbed my arm and swung me into the kitchen.

"Enough, you two," said Mom, setting our plates on the table. Stew, tossed salad with apples and nuts, and corn bread. "Nice dinner, Mom." There. I meant it and you couldn't start an argument with that.

Mom smiled. "Thanks. I like weekends when I have time to cook." Good response.

Tyler was slurping down his stew.

"Where's the fire?" I asked.

He kicked my shin.

"Hey!"

"Okay," warned Mom.

I dipped my bread in the stew.

"Don't play with your food, Hope. Your manners are atrocious. You look like a baby eating with her fingers."

I glanced at Tyler.

"Why do you look at your brother when I'm talking to you?"

Oops. Forgot to be careful. My ears flashed hot.

Mom pointed her fork at Tyler and chuckled. "He's not going to help you out."

You're too late. He already has. Don't you remember Baby Me crying on the sofa and you yelling, "SHUT UP! FOR GOD'S SAKE, SHUT UP!"? And how I just cried louder? And how Tyler climbed onto the sofa and lay next to me, whispering, "Shhh. It's okay. Shhh." If you can't remember, I'll tell you the story he's told me whenever I've felt scared.

I set the dripping corn bread on my plate and stared at the microwave clock. 5:42. Maybe I should wait a minute for a better number. Until then, I'd calculate a few points: 20 for feeling bad, 75 for Mom laughing at me, and 50 for not talking back.

"Did you learn anything this weekend?" Mom asked.

I hesitated. "Yes."

"What?"

This was tricky. I could easily answer, *"I learned that you were once a Nazi prison guard."* Instead, for an additional 20 points, I spoke carefully. "I should keep my mouth shut most of the time . . . and . . . it takes half a box of Tide to wash everything in my room."

Her eyes pierced mine. I stopped breathing. *Funny, Mom, please think I'm funny.*

"Well," she said, all huffy, "just remember this weekend as you walk back and forth to school."

On an angry scale of one to ten, she was probably only a two, so I decided to try my luck. "Can I have my allowance? My room is perfectly clean."

"It means clean *all week*, Hope, not just one day. Plus, you need to do dishes *all* week, too, starting tonight."

"Tyler didn't have to do them last week, so why do I?"

"I —," started Tyler.

"He's in high school now, with lots of homework," Mom said, standing up, which meant the conversation was over.

"I have lots of homework, too."

"Don't whine, Hope," she said, walking out of the kitchen.

End of discussion. Turn your back and leave the room. Fifteen points.

Tyler silently cleared the table, stacking the plates and bowls in the sink. He even wiped off the table, then tossed the sponge in my face.

"Hey!" I wiped my face on my sweatshirt. "Don't you have homework?"

"Oh, yeah, almost forgot." He wandered into the hall. "Lots of it!"

CHAPTER 10

#8726

Monday was the longest day. I couldn't wait to get home, grab my Next to New clothes, and race back to the store. I kept thinking about everything I'd ironed, hung up, and hid in my closet. I couldn't keep my mind on math; instead, I did my own figuring, adding what I'd make from my clothes and shoes, two belts, a stocking hat, and a pair of mittens.

"What were signs of hatred and intolerance toward the Jewish people?" Mr. Hudson's words made me feel guilty for counting my money, when Holocaust victims had everything taken from them. Once more I was inside *Life Is Beautiful* and the concentration camp, rooting for Joshua and his point system.

Brody remembered the sign in the bakery window and on Guido's bookstore door.

"Right," said Mr. Hudson, "but signs aren't always written. Like when daffodils bloom — they're a sign that spring is on the way."

"Like a clue," said Annette.

Mr. Hudson nodded. "What were some clues that the Jews were heading for trouble?"

"The Nazi soldiers marching into town?" said Peter.

"Yes," said Mr. Hudson. "And what about the two men taking Guido from his bookstore to see a city official?"

"Yeah," said Peter again, "and the one guy smashing his cigarette on Guido's window."

"Good observation, Peter. Now, if you could use only one word to say what this movie was about, what would it be?"

I heard "racism," "courage," "survival," "bravery," and "Holocaust." I thought of Guido's wife, Dora (*Principessa*, as he called her), who wasn't Jewish, who raced to the railway station and insisted on boarding the crowded boxcar. I thought of Guido, trying with all his might to save Joshua, to protect him from the horror and give him hope, and, in the end, sacrificing his own life for his wife and son. My eyes watered as I saw Joshua wearing a helmet and riding atop the army tank. And I choked as I heard his ecstatic cry, "Mama!"

"What?" asked Mr. Hudson to the silent room. "Was that you, Hope? Can you say it again, a bit louder this time? What one word describes this movie?"

"Love."

2:55. I dashed from the classroom, out the school doors, alongside buses, down the sidewalk, and past a zillion houses. Out of breath, I fumbled for the key in my backpack, jammed it into the lock, and flung open the door. Storming into my bedroom, I slammed on the brakes. I stood, frozen, staring.

My room. It looked awesome. For a moment, I sucked up all that tidiness, then announced: "100 points."

With my clothes on hangers slung over one arm and

a bag full of shoes and stuff on the other arm, I maneuvered back through the house, out the door, and down the sidewalk. Now my feet barely touched the ground. My body was light and airy. I watched cars pass and wondered if the drivers had any idea that I, Hope Elliot, was on a mission, that I was about to make a great business deal. I smiled.

Then panic hit. What if Mom came home early and saw me? Or someone told her I was hauling half the house away? I slowed my feet and my heart to a regular pace, my legs swish-swishing against the bag, but as soon as I spotted Next to New, my heart shot into double time. My eyes ached to see those purple hiking boots with the thick, black, sturdy soles. *Please, God, let them still be there.*

NO! They weren't in the window! Die. I was going to die.

Someone opened the PULL door for me, and I huffed and puffed my way back to the consignment counter.

Anita was sorting through a lady's resale clothes.

"Did you sell my purple hiking boots?" I blurted. "Sorry," I added as the lady looked at me with squinchy eyebrows. For a split second it seemed Anita didn't remember me or the boots or last Friday. *Remember. Please!!*

"Oh, yes, the boots." She smiled. "I thought you'd be back, so I went ahead and put them on our layaway shelf."

Relief saved me from passing out.

"Here, let me help," said Anita, reaching for my clothes.

"I'm fine," I said, trying to look cool. The second Anita turned, I dropped my bag to the floor. *Oh, my arms!*

The lady left and Anita took my hanging bundle and arranged it on a tall clothes rack. "Now, let's set you up with an account." She clicked the computer mouse. "Name?"

"Hope Marie Elliot." I stood straight and tall, my feet tightly together, my hands at my sides, my eyes fixed on Anita's pumpkin earrings.

After entering my address and phone number, Anita asked, "If some of your clothes are stained or out of style or don't sell after a few months, would you like us to donate them to a local charity?"

I hadn't expected that question. I'd figured all my stuff would sell.

"The churches in town come by for —"

"Yeah," I cut her off, "it's okay."

While Anita typed, I glanced at my hanging clothes. I felt a strange mix of pride and sadness, saying good-bye to part of my life, a part that might live again on some little kid's head or feet. But how would I feel when I saw that bit of memory walking around town or on the playground? And just what kind of memory would it be?

Anita pulled a pen from her hair, now looking redder instead of oranger. She wrote on a small card. "Your membership number is 8726."

8726. A good number. Anita had even written my name in beautiful cursive lettering. It was official. I was a member. I even had a card to prove it. Did that mean

I could live at Next to New? Sleep in a changing room, curled up on the small bench, covered with —

"What about your down payment?"

I'd almost forgotten. I stuffed my hand in my jeans pocket and pulled out two crumpled dollar bills plus eighty cents.

Anita typed again. "That leaves eleven dollars and twenty cents. Can you have that in two weeks?"

Could I bug Mom for my allowance? Collect pop cans? Babysit? Nothing sounded very hopeful.

As if reading my mind, Anita said, "We have a Fifty-Fifty promotion going on right now." She held a bunch of narrow yellow papers. "Write your name on the back of these coupons and give them to all your friends and family. They'll get fifty percent off one item in the store and you'll receive fifty cents credit."

I nodded okay as I saw yellow coupons and shiny coins pouring from the sky, piling around me.

Anita set my purple boots on the counter. "I thought you'd like to see them — you know, visiting rights." She chuckled.

They looked beautiful. I picked them up and rubbed my hand across their tops and bottoms. I fingered the leather laces. I longed to put them on and wear them home. Setting them back on the counter, I smiled at Anita. It was time to earn money: $11.20.

CHAPTER 11

50-50 Club

I smiled. I smiled all the way home. I smiled at the six pop cans I picked up along the way. I especially smiled when I discovered my key to the kitchen door still stuck in the lock and Mom not home yet.

I tried to hide my smile at dinner, working to look all sad about my life, but Tyler was telling funny stories about football practice and Mom was laughing.

My smile stopped when I returned to my bedroom and pulled out my Holocaust homework — a drawing of a concentration camp. I sharpened my colored pencils, not that there'd be much color in this. From Mr. Hudson's descriptions, I added sorting sheds where prisoners' belongings were divided into piles of clothes, shoes, jewelry, books, and toys. Using a ruler, I carefully drew the watchtowers and wooden fence, adding rolls of barbed wire to the top. I lined up prisoners for watery soup and the bathrooms. German soldiers marched with their stiff legs high in the air. Then I decided to put in something that probably wasn't there — a red rosebush — honoring all the Jewish prisoners who shed their blood. Maybe those poor Jews would have looked at that rosebush for hope. Maybe they would have given it a few spare drops of water, keeping it alive one more day. I think Anne Frank would have liked this; she was always looking for little things in her own hidden prison to be happy about, like a sliver of blue sky sneaking through a crack in the curtain or an extra ration of butter during the holidays.

The next morning I walked into the classroom wondering if my nervous heart was banging too loud. The Next to New yellow coupons were safe in a clear, zipped plastic bag, and I'd made a sign-up sheet with the title

"NEXT TO NEW SPECIAL COUPONS," using bright red and yellow markers. I'd even found a clipboard and tied a red pen to it with a piece of string.

But now what? Kids were still arriving, storing lunches, checking the First Things First board. Jessica, Katie, and Lauren sat in a circle on the floor, designing their geodesic domes; Brody and Justin were studying the World War II map.

I sat at my desk, pulled out the coupon bag and clipboard, and began numbering the chart, wishing names would suddenly appear, filling the empty spaces. I went all the way down the page, thirty lines. What was I thinking? What thirty people would want these coupons?

"What's that?" Annette stood next to my desk, pointing at the clipboard.

My chest grabbed, but I faked cool. "The Fifty-Fifty Club. Want to join?"

"How?"

I unzipped the plastic bag and took out one yellow coupon. "It's worth fifty percent off one thing at Next to New." I smoothed out my sign-up chart, knowing

Annette would love all the tidy lines and numbers. We used to play bank in kindergarten — she'd fill out the deposit slips and I'd run the cash register.

"If you want to join, sign your name on line number one."

"I don't know about Next to New," she said cautiously. "Isn't it just old, leftover clothes?" Her nose crinkled.

I pulled out the page of instructions. "It says they have to be in really good condition. I've seen the stuff — it's awesome. And fantastically low prices." I sounded like a car commercial.

Annette eyed the yellow coupon. "Well, I suppose it's okay. My mom loves half-off sales."

"Do you want to sign her up, too?"

She shrugged. "I guess." Annette picked up the red pen and carefully printed her name, and then her mother's on line two. I slipped one more coupon out of the bag, signed my name to the back of both, and handed them to Annette. Now she looked excited, probably because she had something to share with her mother. Before I could feel jealous or sad, Jessica and Lauren were standing there, rattling off questions, saying how they'd sold clothes at Next to New. Lines three and four, please.

"I love that store." It was Brody. My eyeballs practically popped out. Brody *loves* Next to New? Brody Brinkman, Mister Dressed in his Gap khakis, collared shirts, and V-necked sweaters?

"Yeah, it's great," he said, now sounding like Mister Gap Salesman. "My mom shops there all the time. She made it a game when I was a little kid, searching for the best bargain. Now I go in sometimes just to find a sweet deal. I'll really make points when I tell her about this sale."

Before you could say "fifty percent off," Brody had a yellow coupon in one hand and a pen in the other. Line five, please.

CHAPTER 12

Surviving Should

"They're all gone!"

Anita frowned and stopped tagging a pair of pajamas. "What's all gone?"

"The coupons," I answered. A bunch of fourth grade girls at recess had gone crazy, dying to hold the clipboard and sign their names.

"Ah," she said, smiling. "What a saleswoman. Good job."

Good job. The words echoed in my ears as I looked around the store. Only a few customers at 3:16 on a Tuesday afternoon.

The bell above the door jangled and in walked Brody with his yellow coupon. That was fast. Maybe he really did love this place. He glanced around, then saw me and combed his fingers through his hair.

I leaned back against the counter.

He made his way to the rear of the store. "Hey," he said, dropping his backpack to the floor. "There was a Calvin Klein sweater here a few weeks ago, but" — he glanced toward Anita, who was busy tagging again — "it was too much money," he whispered.

I nodded.

"This helps." He held up the coupon. "I hope it's still here."

I nodded again. I felt like I should be directing him, but I had no idea where anything was, except for lay-away boots.

Brody picked up his backpack and gave a slight wave, then headed off toward the front corner.

"Do you have a few minutes to spare?" Anita handed me another stack of yellow discount coupons.

My mind clicked off the minutes: Tyler, football practice, home at 5:30. Mom, 5:45 if she stopped at the store. I checked the wall clock. 3:20. "Sure."

"I'm minus a gal today. How's your ironing?"

"Ironing? I thought everything came in ironed."

"We touch up special items — prom dresses, expensive shirts, whatever. The high school Homecoming dance is in a few weeks, so all the fancy clothes need to look extra fancy. They're in the back." She motioned to the storage room. "Just remember — low heat. Would you mind? I'll deduct five dollars from your hiking boots."

Five dollars. "I'm a great ironer."

The Next to New dresses were all shapes, lengths, sizes — a short, sparkly black dress with spaghetti straps; a red and green plaid crinkly skirt and matching blouse; a simple peach-colored long dress, almost like a nightgown; plus some silky pants and ruffly tops.

Now I wasn't so sure. I mean, I'd done piles of pants and shirts, but what if I put a huge iron hole through one of these gorgeous things? What if I had to pay for it? I sucked in a deep breath, blew it out, and spit on the iron. A low-heat iron should only produce a quiet sizzle, while high-heat spit makes snaps, crackles, and pops. Yup. Quiet sizzle. Good to go.

I arranged the black dress on the ironing board, wondering who had owned it and why they'd given it up. Like a ship, the iron glided across the flowing fabrics and I floated across a decorated gym. I saw myself in each dress as I pressed, smoothed, turned, hung, snapped, and zipped. Now all I needed were shoes, jewelry, and a date.

"Looks good." Anita poked her head in the doorway. She held up a yellow coupon and flipped it over, showing my name. "Calvin Klein sweater."

Five dollars for ironing and fifty cents from Brody's coupon. That left only $3.05 between my hiking boots and my feet.

I looked past Anita and scanned the store.

"He left a few minutes ago," she said.

Warm, warmer, warmest. (My ears.)

"He's nice." Anita flipped off the light in the storage room. "And he brings in good clothes."

Even though I'd done years of my own washing and ironing, I hadn't fixed things like rips or missing buttons. Neither had Mom or Tyler, so the pink plastic sewing basket bulged high and wide with bits of sad shirts and shorts and pants poking through narrow slots like prisoners waving to be rescued. I'd outgrown more orphaned outfits crammed in that overflowing basket.

With the house still to myself, I hauled the basket to my room and dumped the mound on my bed like a pail of packed sand. I began sorting — Tyler, Mom, me, Mom, me, me, Tyler, Mom. It looked like most of my stuff had button problems. I found the button box and pawed through it, matching colors and sizes, then picked thread and a needle.

That night at dinner I decided to break the news. I hadn't said one thing yet about the Fifty-Fifty Club or the clothes I was taking to Next to New, but the purple boots were going to come home soon and they needed an explanation.

"I'm president of the Fifty-Fifty Club." The words nearly clogged my throat.

"What's that?" Mom asked, buttering her roll.

So far, so good.

"Next to New — the resale clothing store on Main Street," I said, my words racing to catch up with my pounding heart. "They have this deal where you can give out these discount coupons and whoever brings them in gets fifty percent off anything and you get fifty cents credit." I gulped for air.

"What possessed you to step foot in that disgusting store?" Mom set her knife down. "And how in the world did you get conned into a sales scheme? I'll bet those secondhand people spotted a real sucker when you walked in. How could you be so clueless, Hope?"

I shrugged. Now my heart banged in my ears like a band of miniature drums.

"How does the store know you get the credit?"

"I write my name on the back of the coupon before I give it to someone." I could barely hear myself over the drums.

"Isn't that just great? Your name is spread all over

Eola Hills." She waved her roll through the air. "I suppose you put our phone number and address on it, too, so we'll get crank calls and strangers at the door." Her jaw set tight. "When will you ever think before you act?"

Tyler cleared his throat, but it didn't catch Mom's attention.

Mom kept on. "You should have a code or a stamp instead of your name. The store should have thought that one through. I'm going to call them."

"No!"

Mom stared.

"I mean — please don't call." I paused, scrambling for words. "It's okay, really. I'm only giving them to kids at school. Really. They're not 'spread all over Eola Hills.'"

"Don't mimic me, Hope."

"I'm not, Mom. Honest." PLEASE LET THIS END. NOW.

I decided not to tell about my clothes, but I still had to mention the boots. "The credit is going for a pair of hiking boots."

"Hiking boots?"

I cringed.

"Sweet," said Tyler. "You'll need 'em for Outdoor School."

My eyes melted into Tyler's. He winked.

"Hope," Mom said firmly, "those boots have been worn by someone else. Probably several someones. You'll get athlete's foot or some strange disease and I don't have the time or the money to take you to the doctor. I don't want those boots in this house."

"Please, Mom, please, I really, really want them. I promise I'll keep them in the garage." Now I was begging for my life.

"You should save your money for a brand-new pair. Check the ads. They have sales all the time. You should get a better deal in the long run."

"But, Mom, these boots look like they've never been worn. I put them on layaway and I only have three dollars and five cents left to pay."

"You shouldn't put anything on layaway, Hope." Now

she was eating her roll. That slowed my heart. "If you don't pay it off on time, poof! There goes your hard-earned money. You should wait until you have the whole amount, then go in, buy it, and bring it home that same day."

"I'll have the money in time so I won't lose a penny." *PLEASE* let this be over.

"Well, throw your money away if you want." Yes. Sarcasm, loud and clear (35 points), which always meant she was winding down and I could go ahead with my plan.

"I sure wouldn't spend my money that way." She shivered. "You wouldn't catch me dead in that store. Remember, Hope, you should start with new, not Next to New." She chuckled at her own cleverness.

Should, Should, Should. I hated *should.* It made me feel stupid. Really stupid. SHOULD needed points: 60. And, I still needed a Grand Prize.

As I watched Mom still making fun of me, my boots, and my coupons, it finally came to me:

CONGRATULATIONS!

* * *

YOU'VE REACHED THE 5,000
POINT GRAND TOTAL.

FROM THIS POINT FORWARD,
YOUR MOTHER, D.D. ELLIOT,
WILL NO LONGER SAY MEAN,
HURTFUL THINGS, AND
YOU WILL NO LONGER
REQUIRE A POINT SYSTEM.

* * *

CHAPTER 13

Tangled Memories

The button-sewing project took a few days, along with washing and drying. I still hadn't said anything about my clothes going to Next to New, not that I was doing anything wrong. They were my clothes, after all. And I certainly couldn't wear them anymore. It's just that I got such a sick feeling whenever I thought I should tell Mom something. I knew exactly how it'd go: The minute I opened my mouth, I would've made all the wrong decisions, I'd be *should*ed to death, and I'd feel super stupid and guilty afterwards.

So, I kept pretty quiet, sewing in my closet, sneaking into the laundry room while Mom watched TV or talked on the phone. I didn't want to chance ironing; I planned to haul wrinkled clothes, in hopes of ironing them at Next to New.

The day our Holocaust project was due, I carefully rolled my concentration camp map, slipped rubber bands around each end, and placed it on a soft bed of out-grown dresses, skirts, and blouses, packed in Tyler's old Nike sports bag. With a few T-shirts and pants tucked along the sides, the map looked safe. My backpack hid the remaining clothes. I tried to convince myself I wasn't a thief, but my heart thought differently, shouting out confessions as I walked through the kitchen.

"Bye, Mom," I said, wishing the door closer.

"What's in the bag?" She started the dishwasher and wiped her hands on the towel.

I froze.

"Uh, it's my concentration camp map. Due today. I don't want it to get wet — since I have to walk." I guarded my voice. Not one hint of sarcasm. 50 points.

"And it's well-padded so it won't get squashed." I gave the side of the bag a gentle pat and moved again for the door. My ears prayed for silence.

"Good luck," said Mom.

Good luck! Better than silence! I couldn't believe it.

"Thanks."

Out the door and down the driveway. I reached the sidewalk and my knees turned to mush. I had to force each leg forward, one at a time, for a few steps until some strength returned. With a misty drizzle dusting my face, I ran, jogged, and fast-walked to school. It made me think of Anne Frank, who walked away from her home forever in a steady rain, wearing layers of clothing, trying to disguise pants, vests, and stockings so the Nazis wouldn't suspect she was going into hiding.

When Mr. Hudson called for the maps, I slowly removed mine from its protective cocoon and carried it like long-lost treasure back to my desk. I slipped the rubber bands off and spread the map, smoothing it flat, my fingers moving gently across drab wooden barracks and dark smoky skies, guard towers and garbage dumps, yellow stars on striped shirts and red blooms on the lone rosebush.

When Mr. Hudson picked it up, I could tell he was

being careful, too. "Nice job, Hope," he said. I tried not to smile. Be cool. *Nice job.* That might even be better than *good job.* I wasn't sure. I'd have to think about it.

I had so many things on my mind that day, it wasn't until afternoon that I noticed Brody's sweater. My eyes moved up the brown and creamy white sleeve to his face. "Next to New," he mouthed from across the room, pulling at the elbow. He gave me a thumbs-up and my ears turned hot.

The bell jingled as I pushed open Next to New's heavy door. I waved to Jodi Huffman, the high-school girl who worked after school three days a week.

Anita was in SHOES.

"Hi," I said, sitting down on the bench.

She tossed a pair of pink fuzzy slippers into a reject pile. "Pink isn't selling these days."

I picked up the slippers and smoothed the helter-skelter hair. "They need mowing."

Anita chuckled. "You do lawns, too?"

"No, just ironing." I returned the slippers to the pile, stalling for time, mentally rehearsing my request. *Would it be okay, that is, could I please use the —*

"What's on your mind?" she asked, sitting down beside me.

I bent over and unzipped the black bag.

"Whoa," said Anita. "Yours?"

I nodded.

"Cute." She pulled out my all-time favorite sunflower sundress with matching hat. When I outgrew the dress, I wore it as a top with pants.

"They're all washed and I checked for stains and fixed rips and sewed buttons, and I know they're supposed to be ironed." The words stumbled over my nervous tongue.

Anita stood up, handing me the dress and hat. "Be sure to fill the iron with bottled water, and use the smaller, children's hangers." She gathered her pile of reject shoes and slippers. "No rest for the wicked." She winked and I hoped she wasn't talking about me.

I passed through my childhood again — smoothing,

folding, and pressing memories: second-grade overalls so hard to undo that I peed in them more than once; a red flowery crop top too short during a time I wanted everything tucked in; a day at the beach in my blue shorts and sailboat T-shirt, when Mom built a sand castle with Tyler and me; a trip to the Eugene Zoo in Mickey Mouse sweats when Mom called me clumsy and clueless after I tripped down the stairs leading to the monkeys; Jessica Dobie's birthday party in my Winnie The Pooh dress and matching apron when Mom wished me a good time.

Why do happy memories come tangled with sad ones? Why can't you just pull out the good ones and leave the bad behind? Is it better to forget them all or remember them all? That was definitely a problem in need of a solution.

Anne took these things into hiding: her diary, hair curlers, handkerchiefs, schoolbooks, a comb, old letters. She wrote, "I put in the craziest things with the idea that we were going into hiding. But I'm not sorry, memories mean more to me than dresses."

CHAPTER 14

New Friends

Saturday afternoon was quiet. Mom was at Tyler's football game and I was studying Anne Frank's diary for a test. Tyler said I was on his blacklist for staying home and that I'd better ace the test.

I took a break and wandered down to Tyler's room. Surely he had some outgrown clothes. I started with his chest of drawers, pulling out stuff I hadn't seen in years — sweatshirts, basketball T-shirts, football jerseys. The prize, though, was these jungle pajamas with lions and tigers, elephants, and parrots. Way too small. Besides, now he wore boxers and T-shirts to bed.

The phone rang. I dived across Tyler's rumpled bed and grabbed the receiver. "Hello."

"Hope?"

"Yes."

"There's a pair of purple hiking boots here with your name on them."

"Anita?"

"Yes, sweetie. I thought you'd like to know. A bunch of your coupons came in today. Your boots are paid off and you even have fifty cents' credit."

Purple hiking boots AND credit.

"I'll be there in a second."

I tore out of Tyler's room and snatched my tennis shoes off the back porch, hopping and tying my laces all at once.

In a flash, I was breathlessly leaning against Next to New's front door, allowing someone coming out to let me in. A fresh surge of anticipation swept me to the back counter, where I was sucked into a crowd of closet cleaners.

"Hope. Back here." Anita signaled from the storage room.

I weaved out of the crowd and slipped behind the counter.

Anita whipped the boots out from behind her back, holding them in midair, her grin glowing in her eyes. "Put them on."

I kicked off my shoes. She quickly loosened the leather laces and pulled out the purple tongues. I bent over and tried cramming my feet in. *Slow down.* I sat on the floor and carefully pulled the laces tight, one row at a time, then tied them in a double-knotted bow. Anita helped me up and we examined the finished look. "Perfect," she said.

Like Miss America taking her runway walk, I stood tall and gazed out across the audience of winter coats, men's suits, and maternity tops. Then I strolled past restrooms, dressing rooms, and the kiddie play corner. It's hard to be Miss America, though, when you're staring at your feet.

Back at the storage room, Anita and Ruthie were examining a white sweater, but they stopped as soon as they saw me.

"They're gorgeous," said Ruthie.

"As good as you remember?" asked Anita.

"Better." This must be heaven. Next to New and new-to-me boots.

Anita returned to the sweater. "What do you think, Hope? Is the stain noticeable?"

Ruthie handed me the sweater and I held it in different directions under the ceiling light. "Well," I hesitated, "it's not as bad in the shadows, but in bright light, I can see it. I probably wouldn't buy it." I raised my eyebrows, wondering if I'd answered okay, and gave the sweater back.

"I'd agree," Anita said. Ruthie nodded.

They must be good friends, I thought, glancing from Anita's XXL Halloween sweater to Ruthie's, then back to their ears. Tiny ghosts dangled from Anita's, witches on broomsticks swung from Ruthie's. And the hair color thing. Anita's now verged on red-red instead of orange-red. Ruthie seemed wrinkly enough for gray hair, but hers was as black as licorice.

"So, Hope," said Ruthie, flopping the white sweater over her shoulder, "I understand you're quite the saleswoman and we're going to go broke with all these discount coupons flying in here."

I grinned, even though I wasn't sure how much to believe.

"Congratulations, darlin'. I suppose that yellow ski jacket in the window is next on your list."

I smiled. "Maybe," I said. Yellow and purple, a perfect combination. "I'd better get home — I have a test Monday."

Ruthie put her arm around my shoulder. "You take good care of those boots, now."

"I will."

"Check in with me next week, Hope," said Anita. "There might be some more ironing."

I rolled my eyes, pretending I was annoyed. Anita chuckled and something nudged my brain, like a baby chick poking at its shell, wanting out.

"See you later," I said, looking at them a moment longer.

"Bye," they said in unison, their earrings jangling.

I walked down the street, my tennis shoes in a paper bag, my purple boots strong against the pavement, and my thoughts on two crazy ladies who seemed to like me. I wondered if they lived together, and if I'd have to dye my hair in order to live with them.

I took a deep breath of cool fall air and picked out the hint of smoke from someone's leaves burning. One of my favorite smells. It was a good day. A Number 6 Day.

CHAPTER 15

Climbing Mountains

Later that afternoon I sat cross-legged on Tyler's bedroom floor, a pile of his little boy clothes in front of me.

"I've got a business deal for you."

"What? You sell my clothes and you get the money?" He lay on his bed tossing a basketball in the air.

"No, smarty. I wash, iron, sew up rips, take everything on hangers to Next to New, and we split the money."

"Plus ten bucks for snooping through my stuff!"

"I wasn't snooping. I was just getting a head start."

He climbed off the bed, throwing the basketball in my lap. "Then let's get serious." He stood in front of his opened closet and began tossing Wrangler jeans and silver-buckled belts and long-sleeved Western shirts my way. "No more cowboy dress-up. I'm through playing the Lone Ranger." He even pulled out his really nice suede boots. Totally sweet. They should go for a great price.

"Tyler," I said hesitantly. He turned around. "I don't know what Mom would say, so I'm keeping this kinda quiet. Okay?"

"That'll be another ten bucks."

"No way!" I aimed his basketball at him.

"All right." He held his hands up. "But don't expect me to bail you out when you get caught."

"I won't get caught." I smiled and lowered the ball.

"How exactly do you plan to sneak this stuff out?" he asked, his head back in the closet.

"I have my ways."

With Tyler's clothes hiding in my closet, I tried studying again for my test. I shuddered, wondering if I could have endured Anne Frank's hidden prison and the constant fear of being found, aching for a breath of fresh air, craving to eat anything besides potatoes and beans. I skimmed the pages, feeling Anne's frustrations with her mother's mean words, the longing for friends, the deadly silence.

Monday morning I finally rode the bus again. It had only been a week, but it seemed forever. I lugged Tyler's old Nike sports bag and my backpack to the middle of the bus. Dropping my stuff next to a free window, I sat down on the plastic seat. Tyler slowed as he passed by, heading for the back with the other high schoolers. He eyed his bag. "Whatcha stealin'?" he whispered loudly.

"*Tyler.*" I scowled. "No half for you!"

"I'll tell."

"No, you won't!"

Noelle Laslett got on at the next stop, sat down beside me, and opened her jacket. "I got these overalls at Next to New."

"Good find," I said.

"Only five dollars with my coupon." She grinned.

And your coupon helped buy my boots, I thought,

moving them on the rubber mat: heel, toe, heel, toe, climbing Lava Butte.

I held my breath as Mr. Hudson passed out the test, the paper turned over, silent questions daring me to remember.

"You have twenty minutes," he said.

I expected to see true-false, multiple choice, fill in the blank, but instead there was only one question: "How does the following story compare to the Holocaust? A frog jumped into a pan of very hot water and instantly jumped back out. Another frog jumped into a pan of cold water that slowly got hotter and hotter. The frog adapted to the increasing heat until the boiling water killed him."

I sat there for a moment feeling sick about the dead frog, then my mind wandered back to Guido, Dora, and Joshua and how they got used to the soldiers on every street corner, the stores closed to Jews and dogs. I thought back to Anne Frank's long list of forbidden freedoms, yet she wrote, ". . . things were still bearable." I remembered her words because I've said similar ones to myself — shut up in my bedroom, writing in my points journal, lying on my closet bed — trying to convince myself that I was okay. Now I looked out the classroom windows to the open fields and wide blue sky. I thought another minute, then began writing.

By the time I finished I was wiped out, but then I thought about Anne Frank, who'd written a million thoughts about the real thing; not just a twenty-minute test, but a twenty-four-hour-a-day test. A survival test. I felt bad for feeling tired.

After Mr. Hudson collected the papers, he began handing back our map projects. I scrunched my toes inside my boots and released them. Scrunched. Released. The wait was killing me. At last, standing beside my desk, Mr. Hudson paused and announced, "Please notice the great care that went into this project." He held up my concentration camp map for the entire class to see. Then, just to me he said quietly, "I like the rosebush." He lowered my map onto my desk like a royal crown.

A+.

What a beautiful letter. Those nice straight, even lines, meeting at the top, the mountaintop. And the prize "+" — the flag at the very tip of the mountain.

CHAPTER 16

Mountain Ranges

One thing about climbing mountains: you have to go back down. That's what my life was doing. Up and down. High and low. One mountain after another. It reminded me of those zigzag graphs coming out of heart-monitoring machines hooked up to hospital patients.

Mr. Hudson was definitely top-of-the-mountain. He was hard, but fair. And funny. For Halloween he painted a smiley pumpkin face on his bald spot and gave us orange glow sticks for Outdoor School. I'd never studied so much, but I wanted to be high on his Good Role Model List, plus I had to make up for that stupid bus referral. I didn't want a single question mark by my name.

I aced my Anne Frank test and left it on Tyler's bed;

it landed back in my room as an airplane with *Proud of You* written across the wings. Our half-book test was more difficult, but smarty Brody and I tied for the highest score.

Another mountaintop: Anita and Ruthie. They could make a sale day out of any occasion — Drizzly Days Deals, Two-for-One Tuesdays, Halloween Surprises — with signs, prizes, and decorations to match. They were the two best friends I'd ever seen. Of course, they'd had a long time to get there; they'd known each other since kindergarten. With both their husbands dead and their kids grown and gone, they'd moved in together and opened Next to New. I wondered if I'd have a lifetime friend, laughing over old memories, hugging and kissing cheeks, giving each other cards and flowers for no reason.

One more mountain high: purple hiking boots, now worn with thick woolly socks, which kept my feet warm even during recess.

In between the highs were the lows — not diving,

crashing, exploding lows, but rather nagging, poking, bugging lows. For instance: Garbage Day, every other Wednesday . . .

"Don't forget to put the . . ." Mom's voice bursts into the bathroom, then fades. I'm clear at the end of the hallway and she's yelling from the kitchen door. I turn off the water and take the toothbrush out of my mouth. "What?" I yell back, watching my eyebrows frown at the mirror.

"*It's garbage day,*" she yells again, this time louder. "*Every other Wednesday. Can't you remember?*"

I hear her voice, but it's like cafeteria rules. Pretty soon you don't hear the thousandth-time reminder words.

"***Hope, you stupid shit! Answer me!***" The words echo in my ears.

"Yeah, I know." I probably should yell louder, too, but I've lost all my yelling energy. It comes out a medium mumble. I turn the water back on and rinse my toothbrush.

"Hope Marie, get your dumb ass down here right now and take out the goddamn garbage!"

I sigh and inch my head out the door. Now she's standing halfway down the hall, her hands on her hips, her lips pressed tight.

"I'm just finishing my teeth." The words limp out, filling an excuse.

"I know you're going to forget." She's not yelling now, but the words are just as loud.

"I won't. I promise."

Garbage day. Every other Wednesday.

Another low: INTERRUPTING. Take Thanksgiving dinner, for instance. Mom's friend Lydia Bishop came over, which was good because she's nice. I passed the mashed potatoes and she asked how I was doing and what was new, but when I opened my mouth to answer, Mom's words came out. "She'll be lucky to make it through sixth grade."

Lydia smiled at me and tried again. "What are you doing in your spare time?" My lips parted and once more Mom's voice was there: "Hope is spending way too much time at that consignment store. Anyone for more turkey?" Conversation over. Onto pumpkin pie recipes and Christmas sales, and I quietly returned to my cranberry salad.

There was something new grinding at my life: headaches. I think they started that day in Mrs. Piersma's office. While I was concentrating on the peppermints, I noticed a pain in my jaw traveling up to my eyes and across my forehead. After that, they came more often, sometimes with a little warning, other times flying in out of nowhere. I'd be sitting in class, thinking about morning math, and *wham*. The pounding in my brain would start right while I was figuring miles from Seattle to San Francisco. The numbers blurred and nothing made sense. Or the pain would start behind my eyes, like someone had tied them into tight knots and was pulling them deep inside my head. Even my teeth hurt. Yeah, my teeth. Tops and bottoms, like I'd been chewing ten pieces of bubble gum for ten days straight.

If I complained about the pain, Mom gave me two aspirin and told me I shouldn't have headaches at my age. Sleeping used to help, but then I began waking up in the morning with a headache. How do you get a headache sleeping?

Highs and lows. Christmas was both. I'd climb up, take in all the beautiful lights and music, the school program, and TV specials. We'd decorate our classroom and have a party with red punch and ice cream, cookies, games, and secret pal gifts.

The low was my mom's belief in Christmas crafts. You know that song, "The Twelve Days of Christmas," with the turtledoves and lords a-leaping? Well, in our house, it was "The Twelve *Crafts* of Christmas," with at least twelve bulging bags from Fancy Fabrics crammed with pillow patterns, tassels, rickracks, sequins, and piles of red and green fabric covered with reindeer, snowmen, and Santas.

I used to get excited about Christmas crafts, but then I got tired of GRABBING — when someone decides you're doing something the wrong way and they're going to show you the *right way,* so they grab whatever you're doing out of your hands, saying, "You should do it this way." (Points Total: *Grabbing + Shoulding + Interrupting + Feeling Stupid* = 385.) I'd avoided the dining room workshop for years, but there was still crafty stuff scattered all over the house — half-finished projects and newly started projects, leaving hardly any room for our own decorations.

The biggest problem was that the closer we got to Christmas, the crabbier Mom got, because none of her projects were done. Most people have a Merry Christmas; we had a Crabby Christmas.

This year, however, Christmas wasn't too bad. We sat around the fake Christmas tree in bathrobes and slippers, drinking hot chocolate, opening presents. I got a basketball from Tyler; gloves, hiking socks, and a bead kit from Mom; twenty-five dollars from Grandma. I gave Tyler two shirts from Next to New. Mom got a warm red scarf that had never been worn. I'm not sure she liked it.

There is one more Christmas high: the day *after*

Christmas — Mom's favorite day of the year. She even says so. She's always cheery and smiley and dancing around the house to Christmas carols, eating fudge and her famous sugar cookies, lazing on the couch with a new book from Lydia. Next year I think I'll give my present to her on December 26.

CHAPTER 17

Rain or Shine?

"Bite together." I closed my mouth.

"Now open." I opened my mouth.

"Hmmm . . . let's see. Uh-huh." Dr. McKillip examined my teeth with his miniature mirror, then set the mirror on a tray hanging behind me and placed his hands on my jaw, moving it up and down, back and forth, pressing the sides of my face above my ears. "Does this hurt?"

"No."

He sat up straight on his stool and crossed his arms over his white jacket. "Well, young lady, I'd like to say you ate too many candy canes this Christmas. That's an easy fix. But it looks like you're grinding your teeth.

Your bicuspids and molars are getting the worst of it."
He pointed to the back of his own mouth, then spoke
to my mother leaning against the doorway. "That'll certainly cause her teeth to hurt and can bring on the headaches, too."

He turned back to me and looked right into my eyes.
"Hope," he said quietly, like we were the only two people in the entire office, "how are you doing?"

A strange mix of panic and pride rushed over me
while my ears tingled hot. He wanted to know how *I* was
doing? A kid he only sees maybe once a year? My eyes
turned misty and my throat was so tight I didn't think I
could talk.

"Hope Marie," came my mother's words, "answer Dr.
McKillip."

He gave her a sharp glance, then his eyes softened
again as they studied mine. "Are you under any unusual
stress at school?"

"Just regular stuff," I managed to say.

"There's no way she can be stressed," said Mom.
"She's only in sixth grade. She's just too sensitive. If

anyone should be grinding their teeth, it should be *me*. I've been stressed out for as long as I can remember."

Dr. McKillip frowned and looked out the window. "Mrs. Elliot," he said, studying the bare tree and hanging bird feeders, "I would be more than happy to examine your teeth for a grinding problem. You're welcome to make an appointment before you leave."

He turned his head and spoke to me again. "So everything's okay at school?"

"Yeah."

He shifted around on his seat. "Uh, what about outside of school — anything bothering you?"

"She doesn't have a thing to be bothered about," said Mom, now standing in the middle of the doorway. "Like I said, she's only eleven years old."

Dr. McKillip patted my arm and stood up with a sigh. "I see many stressed-out eleven-year-olds, Mrs. Elliot. They may not have the same worries you or I do, but kids can be extremely concerned about a lot of things. You might want to look into this for Hope's sake."

Mom started to say something, then closed her mouth and looked down at the floor.

Dr. McKillip moved to the sink, turned on the water, and began mixing something in a small bowl. "I'm going to make impressions of Hope's teeth and have a special mouthpiece made for her to wear at night in order to protect her teeth and buffer her nerves. We'll be done here in a few minutes, Mrs. Elliot. You're welcome to relax in the waiting room with a cup of hot tea or coffee."

Mom was silent on the way home. Actually, she'd been pretty quiet the past few weeks. "After-Christmas blues," she called it. "Back to the same old routine. Same old, same old." I'd find her staring out the kitchen window while dinner fixings sat waiting on the counter, or she'd lose track of time, brushing her teeth for ten minutes.

"I'm sick and tired of these Oregon winters," she'd said one morning as rain dribbled down the window. "Rain, rain, rain." She snatched a piece of bread out of the toaster and mashed butter on it. "What I'd give for a spot of sun." That's when she'd bring up moving. Southern California, Arizona, New Mexico. Someplace, anyplace where the sky was blue and the sun shined hot.

Well, she could have her sunny California and just leave me home. There's no way I was moving from Mr. Hudson, Anita and Ruthie, or my closet. And that's just where I headed when we got home from the dentist. I turned on the lamp, closed the door, picked up Turtle, and lay down. My entire body melted, my legs turning limp as noodles, my headache fading as my eyes wandered across the closet walls. Now they were covered with magazine pictures of sunflowers and waterfalls, seagulls flying above the ocean, a Christmas tree sparkling with white lights. There were the words to my favorite songs, my old star chart, my A+ Holocaust map, a newspaper picture of Gabriela Feliciano shooting a basket, and a quote from Anne Frank: ". . . I've found that there is always some beauty left — in nature, sunshine, freedom, in yourself; these can all help you."

Curled up in my closet bed, I felt like a bear, hibernating in my dark, safe cave. I closed my eyes and inspected my teeth with my tongue. There were still a few bits of dried guck from Dr. McKillip's impressions. He had me bite into this pile of gooey clay stuff, which was surely going to harden onto my teeth forever. But it was still nice being in his office. After Mom left for the waiting room, he got all chatty, talking about his plans to take his family to Disneyland for spring vacation. He asked if I'd ever been to Disneyland. I shook my head. He kept talking, like we were having this great conversation, with me grunting through gooey clay or nodding my head.

When he walked me to the waiting room, he put his hand on my shoulder and said, "Your mouthpiece will be ready in a week." He gave a quick squeeze. "Hang in there, Hope."

Now I blinked my eyes open and gazed up to the hems and cuffs, buttons and zippers of my hanging clothes. The view had changed. After Christmas, I'd gone through everything one more time, plus Tyler's, and hauled another load to Next to New. Our clothes were selling well, so along with coupon credits and ironing for Anita, I'd bought two pairs of jeans, a sweater, another pair of boots so I could save my purple ones for Outdoor School, and a daisy necklace with matching earrings. And, last but not least, the yellow ski jacket — half-priced in the January Value-Days Sale.

I glanced down the length of my bed to my bookcase, a regular grocery store by now. Whenever I walked home from Next to New, I stopped at Safeway and bought a bag of oyster crackers, cereal bars, canned cheese, red licorice, or green olives. I even found a small electric coffeepot at Goodwill so I could heat water and make hot chocolate or chicken noodle soup.

The bottom shelf was for my library. So far, *Anne Frank: The Diary of a Young Girl* was my only book. We'd finished our Holocaust unit months ago, but we hadn't finished the book. Mr. Hudson said we could borrow it if we wanted to read the second half. At first, I wanted to hurry up and get to the end, but now I was slowing down, figuring if I didn't finish, the Nazis wouldn't find the "Secret Annexe," arrest everyone, and haul them off to concentration camps. Anne Frank wouldn't die if I didn't finish her story.

I wrapped Turtle in my arms, nestled back into my pillow, and with the golden glow of lamplight falling softly on my eyes, I could see Dr. McKillip again, his hand on my shoulder. I could feel his gentle touch and hear his angel voice. I let the tears come. They pressed out the sides of my eyes, wandered into my hair and down to my ears, tickling as they turned cold. I wiped them away with Turtle's foot.

I wished I had a father like Dr. McKillip. If Mom moved to California, maybe I could move to Dr. McKillip's office. I'd have plenty of toothbrushes and little sample toothpastes, plus a bed on that big dental lounge chair.

CHAPTER 18

Name It and Tame It

Mrs. Nelson, our school counselor, stood in front of the classroom and slipped Paper Bag Patty over her hand. The puppet was freshly colored with crayon-yellow hair, black eyes, and a smiley red mouth. A big purple heart covered her brown chest.

"Remember first grade? Sitting in a circle on the floor, passing around Paper Bag Patty?" Mrs. Nelson's own black eyes moved from face to face, her pink mouth serious.

"Yeah," said Noelle. "We crumpled her every time we said something that hurt her feelings."

"Like what?" said Mrs. Nelson, bobbing Patty's head in time with her words.

"Moron," said Colin Davis.

Mrs. Nelson grabbed Patty's purple heart and squished it tight.

"Pimple face," said Annette.

Again, Mrs. Nelson twisted and wrinkled the puppet's body.

"Loser," "fatty," "dork," came the names, along with more crushes and creases.

"Stupid," I said, my own heart squeezing tight, sending a silent "sorry" to Patty.

By now you couldn't see any of the colors, just this brown wadded clump like a used lunch sack about to be tossed in the garbage.

"Then we tried to smooth out the lines," said Mrs. Nelson, "by saying nice things like 'smart,' 'awesome,' 'cool.'" Mrs. Nelson's fingers massaged Patty's heart, head, and body, unable to completely erase the wrinkles. "What was left behind?"

"Slime," said Brody.

"Right," said Mrs. Nelson, removing Patty, setting her

on Mr. Hudson's desk. "Hurting words are slugs that slime our hearts. What else?"

"Scars." I felt my mouth move and heard the word as if it had helped itself out.

Mrs. Nelson looked at me for a moment, then took a deep breath and placed her hands on her hips. "As sixth graders, you are ready to call hurting, sliming, scarring words what they really are." She paused.

Everyone got extra quiet and leaned forward, waiting to share the sixth-grade secret.

"Abuse. It's verbal abuse."

Now her right hand jabbed the air above our heads. "Verbal abuse is *as* damaging as physical abuse, or worse. It takes twenty-five to thirty positive comments to overcome the effects of one abusive comment. The scars from verbal abuse run just as deep, if not deeper, than physical scars."

With her strong words still hanging in the air, she assured us with softer words that it was important to properly name something. "When you name it, you tame it.

It's like putting a fence around a wild animal so you're safe to learn about it." Then she gave us words to help in abusive situations — *I feel* words, asking-for-a-change words.

An hour later, I stood in front of Next to New, staring at my reflection against green shamrocks. I couldn't think about St. Patrick's Day, though, with Mrs. Nelson's *abuse* word in my head. Why did she wait until sixth grade to tell us? Little kids should know that hurting words are not only slimy and scarring, but **abusive**. I'd always liked Mrs. Nelson, but now I felt a knot of anger in my stomach. She should have told me sooner.

The knot tightened in my stomach as my mother's own words crashed through my head: *dumb shit, stupid as a stick, hopelessly lazy.* I couldn't believe she was doing something to me that had an official name, like chicken pox or the flu. I could just hear a doctor say, "You have a bad case of verbal abuse."

Now that it had a name it seemed more real, more serious, more important. Did that make me more important, too, in a weird sort of way? You know, like the kid who comes to school after a skiing accident, his leg in a cast, hobbling around with crutches. At first he's famous, everyone feeling sorry for him and a little jealous of all his attention, his cool crutches, someone carrying his books and lunch tray. But after a while, it's actually a bad thing because it probably still hurts and he can't play basketball or get it wet.

I shivered and opened the Next to New door, the bell jangling.

"Hey, sweetie," said Anita. "We're pulling all the purple-tagged clothes." She hauled an armload of winter jackets and sweaters to the *50% Off* rack. "They've had their three months of glory," she said, hanging them back up.

"Think spring," said Ruthie as she dropped unsold sales clothes into a huge laundry basket set on wheels. A man and woman from some church came every Saturday for the leftovers, sending them off to places you see on the news after floods and hurricanes and wars. I kept looking for those pink fuzzy slippers to show up on someone's feet standing in desert sand. Sometimes I wondered if these people really wanted our clothes or if they just wore them for the TV cameras and *National Geographic* pictures.

"I'm selling chocolate candy bars." I held up plain milk chocolate and semisweet with almonds.

"Hope Elliot, you are a tease!" Anita shook her head.

Ruthie rolled her eyes. "Thanks a lot. You show up just when my stomach starts growling." She looked at Anita. "Are we going to be good?"

"What's it for?" asked Anita, like she needed an important cause in order to cheat on her diet.

"Outdoor School." I waved the white-and-gold-wrapped candy in the air. "Super delicious."

Anita shook her head. "Ruthie. We've lost eleven pounds between the two of us and Monday is weigh-in. I've got carrots and apple slices in the back room."

"Are they chocolate-covered?" Ruthie looked like she was in pain.

"How about I leave one for each of you?" I said. "And if you lose another pound by Monday night, you can pay me for them."

"What if we don't?" asked Ruthie.

"Pay me?"

"No — lose the weight?"

"I know," said Anita, "I'll buy the candy bars and *you* eat them, you skinny little thing." She eyed me up and down.

"I can't."

"You can't eat chocolate?" Now Ruthie looked horrified, like I was missing my daily vitamins.

I shrugged. "Dr. McKillip says it might add to my headaches."

Dr. McKillip had bought two candy bars when I'd picked up my mouth guard. "Hold it under warm water to soften it before you put it on. You don't want to break this expensive little number." He nodded toward the bathroom. "Try it before you leave."

I stood at the sink, hot water pouring over the clear plastic mold. Was this how people with dentures felt? Holding their fake teeth in their hands, scrubbing them clean, popping them back in place? Freaky.

I turned off the water, shook the horseshoe-shaped impression, then pushed it up, over my top teeth. It was smooth and thick, forcing my upper lip out, like a monkey.

I returned to the reception room. "I hhink iss okay."

The receptionist smiled while I drooled on the floor.

"You probably don't want to talk on the phone to your boyfriend with that in your mouth," Dr. McKillip said, smiling.

I quickly pulled the guard from my mouth and packed it back in its red container.

He handed me a piece of paper as I walked out the door. "Some headache tips," he said, and raised his hand, waving good-bye.

Now, watching Anita and Ruthie pulling, hanging, and rearranging clothes, I wished I was trying to lose weight rather than shake a headache. I wished I went to their weekly weigh-in meetings (they called it their *support group*). I wished I had someone to talk to, like Ruthie telling Anita she needed a chocolate fix. "Don't eat it," Anita would say. "Throw it away. Go for a walk, sweetie, or drink a glass of water." I wished there was a support group for verbal abuse. I'd go. Even by myself.

CHAPTER 19

Birthday Wishes

From one year to the next I've never known what to expect for my birthday. Some years Mom has made a big fuss with balloons and streamers and my favorite chocolate-fudge cake and a special present like my clock radio. Other years she's given me ten dollars and told me to buy myself a present. When I turned nine, she didn't say a word. My birthday went right on by like a car driving straight through a red light. A few weeks later Tyler asked, "Don't you have a birthday sometime around now?"

Last year Annette and Noelle came over to watch movies and spend the night. I was carrying a huge bowl of popcorn and a plastic bottle of Coke into the living room when I tripped on the rug. Buttered popcorn and fizzing Coke splattered across the floor and furniture.

Annette and Noelle started laughing, but I just stared at the brown spotted ceiling, sick with dread. Before I could pick up the first piece of popcorn, Mom burst into the room. Annette and Noelle stopped laughing.

"You clumsy idiot," said Mom. "Get this cleaned up right now." She looked at Annette and Noelle. "You two call your parents. The party's over."

"But, Mom," I started, heat sweeping my body, burning my ears.

"SHUT UP! And do what you're told!"

With last year's birthday still a nightmare and just a week until my twelfth birthday, I tried to figure out Mom's mood.

"I'm really going to feel older when I'm twelve," I hinted.

"Uh-huh." Mom kept reading the morning paper.

"I'm eleven and I'll be twelve on the thirteenth."

"So?" She glanced up.

"So that's a good sign — three numbers in sequence."

"And your point?"

This wasn't working. But then I remembered the phone call last night from Grandma. I should have known better. Never ask for anything the morning after Grandma calls. Just forget it. The calls came every few months, with Mom trying to be polite to her own mother, but always turning loud and angry with huge sighs and finally shouting, "Don't tell me how I should raise my kids!" and hanging up hard.

I couldn't give up, though, on the birthday business. "This is a really special year since it's my last at the elementary school, so I thought we could do something extra special, you know, maybe a day at the beach, or Night Lights at the Portland Zoo, or paintballing, or —"

"Hope, in case you've forgotten, and I tell you this every year, your birthday comes at our busiest time at work. I don't have the energy to plan a party."

"I'll plan it."

"Not after last year's disaster."

I stood there wondering if I was dismissed, but then she reached for her wallet and slapped twenty-five dollars on the table. "Spend this however you want. Take a friend to a movie and out for pizza. Or buy something. Or save it. Whatever."

Twenty-five dollars. At first I wasn't all that excited about the money. Somehow it felt more like a punishment than a present. Go figure.

But, then, a few days later, I found myself thinking what I could do with it. First I thought of the usual stuff. Then my twenty-five dollars stretched with my imagination: I saw the Humane Society animal ads and I felt a furry soft kitten sleeping next to me. I passed the Eola Hills Travel Agency and was jumping waves in Hawaii. I dreamed of going to a concert, flying in an airplane, a day at Disneyland.

I woke on my birthday still not sure what I was going to do. But I was excited it was Saturday and I still had my twenty-five dollars, even though I'd spent it a million times already in my head.

"Happy birthday, Hope," said Mom, sitting at the kitchen table smoking a cigarette, ads spread across the opened newspaper. "I think Lydia and I are going to hit some of the spring sales today."

I stopped. Her words circled in my ears, faster and louder, spinning and echoing, now snatching chunks of stored conversations: *in case you've forgotten . . . I tell you . . . every year . . . our busiest time at work . . . don't have the energy to plan a party.*

"What about work?" I mumbled.

"Work's fine." Mom squashed her cigarette in a jar lid and began cutting coupons. "We're caught up for now."

I slogged through quicksand to the refrigerator. *It's okay,* my brain tried to reason with me. *It's your birthday and you're twelve. You can do anything you want today. Forget her. It's your birthday and you're okay. Give yourself one hundred points for DISAPPOINTED.*

After choking down a bowl of cereal, I took a shower,

checked out my bare reflection in the full-length mirror (nothing new or different), and put on a skirt, sweater, and my purple hiking boots. As soon as Mom was gone, I crammed my birthday money plus some Next to New earnings into my jacket pocket and walked out the door.

The air was cool and the pavement damp after a night rain, but there were splotches of blue between white and gray clouds. I sucked in the moist air, washing my insides. I wasn't sure where I was going, but my feet turned to town and started walking. The day was mine. All mine.

I stood in front of the Quail Run Bakery, studying row upon row of sprinkle doughnuts, maple bars, blueberry muffins, the fan above the door spreading frosting and coffee smells. In a flash I was walking down the street again, the first taste of a warm, magically sweet cinnamon roll in my mouth.

I passed outdoor coffee drinkers, paper readers, dog walkers, two little girls in ballet tights, a guy parking his motorcycle. The sun was shining warmer now as I studied French beaches, Alaskan cruises, and Mexican ruins taped to the window at Eola Hills Travel Agency. I decided to do all three . . . someday. A little boy and his mom were standing in front of the Hallmark store, giving away kittens. I held a black-and-white fur ball up to my face and closed my eyes as it licked my cheek. I wish. Instead, I found in Hallmark a fuzzy brown-striped stuffed kitten with a pink tongue. Six dollars and it was mine.

By lunchtime, I'd wandered through antique and clothes shops, Tyler's used-to-be-favorite Cowboy Country, shoe stores, and an outdoor garden display with birdbaths and fountains and even a waterfall spilling down into a pond. I sat on a metal bench by the pond and watched huge goldfish wiggle-waggle around each other.

At the Second Street Deli, I ordered three turkey sandwiches and three chocolate-chip cookies. With a few dollars left in my pocket, I carried the white sack and my Hallmark bag down the street, over four blocks, and into Next to New.

The morning shoppers were gone and the closet cleaners hadn't arrived yet. I found Anita and Ruthie studying the Chinese restaurant menu. "But we can't eat the rice," said Anita.

"Just don't eat the fortune cookie," said Ruthie.

"How about turkey?" I said, holding up the sack.

"Hope!" they said together.

"Is a sandwich okay?" I began opening the bag. "You don't have to eat the chips, but you do have to eat the cookies, because they're for my birthday."

"Your birthday?" Ruthie practically shrieked. "But you shouldn't be here on a sunny spring Saturday — you should be out with your friends, shopping or —"

"Stuff it, Ruthie," Anita said, slamming her elbow into Ruthie's side. "Hope came to the right place. Let's celebrate."

Anita hustled us to the storage room and whipped out a card table and three folding chairs, flowery napkins, and the Easter globe off her desk. She cranked the globe key and shook the glitter while Ruthie and I handed out sandwiches, pickles, olives, chips, and chocolate-chip cookies. With "Here Comes Peter Cotton-tail" chiming away, I told them about my twenty-five dollar tour of downtown Eola Hills and passed around my stuffed kitten. "I've always wanted a pet," I said. "I think I'll name him Peter."

"We are honored you and Peter chose to celebrate your birthday luncheon with us," said Anita, raising her Diet Pepsi.

"Absolutely," said Ruthie, standing up, raising her coffee cup. "To Hope and to many more turkey sandwiches."

"Thank you," I said, the cold turkey warming my stomach.

After "Happy Birthday" and the last bite of cookie, Anita announced, "Next to New will match your twenty-five dollars. Consider this your gift certificate." She handed me her napkin with *$25* scribbled across the flowers. "Not exactly fancy wrapped, but you didn't give us much notice."

"Enough notice for next year, though," said Ruthie.

And I knew they wouldn't forget.

CHAPTER 20

Next to New Me

Anita needed sundresses. "Hot fashion for a hot summer."

I'd already taken in my summery things and Tyler warned me to stay out of his clothes. Mom had brought home two new dresses when she'd gone shopping with Lydia (on my birthday), which got me thinking, planning, and waiting for the right moment.

Monday morning, spring vacation, Tyler was still asleep and Mom had left for work. I tiptoed down the hall, past Tyler's bedroom, into Mom's room, and across the floor to her closet. I opened the door. It squeaked and I froze. *Forget it, Hope!* My eyes wandered to Mom's dresser and touched the photo of my baby self, curled in her arms, snuggled against her checkered dress, on that sunny day in March twelve years ago.

I could have stayed in that warm picture forever but reminded myself of the mission and quickly moved through the hanging clothes, stopping at the blue and white homecoming dress. My heart stopped as I grasped the hanger and pulled the dress from the closet.

At Next to New, I tested the iron while Anita fussed at her desk, coughed, glanced at Mom's dress, eyed me, opened and closed drawers, released a loud sigh, then sank down on her chair. "What *else* does your mother want to sell?"

I arranged the dress and began ironing. "Nothing."

"Hmm. That's odd. Most people bring in a pile of things they want to get rid of."

"She's too busy."

"Well, it's a lovely dress. Doesn't look like it's ever been worn."

"It was." I turned the fabric gently, my hands patting,

spreading, resting, longing to hug the blue-and-white-checkered dress one last time.

Anita shook her head and left the room.

Spring break at Next to New turned into a party with the Two-for-One Sale, balloons, door prizes, and food. Ruthie brought in fresh veggies and a great dip she said was low-cal. Anita made low-carb carrot cake that tasted like cardboard. I robbed our garage of diet pop and apples and I bought a new jar of green olives.

I made chocolate-fudge brownies using the cholesterol-free directions, which meant I had to take out the egg yolks — a slimy mess. Instead of frosting, I just sprinkled powdered sugar all over, which looked pretty and *had* to be less calories.

Closet cleaners kept us pretty busy all week, with summer clothes coming in and sale stuff going out. One slower afternoon I was on hanger duty: gathering strays; sorting plastic, wood, wire; taking extras to the storage room. I was tidying the stack behind the consignment counter when a woman's voice drew my head around.

She was talking about the clothes she'd brought in like she knew exactly what we expected.

"Everything's washed and ironed. No stains or rips. It's all good."

There was a hint of something familiar in her voice, how she paused between sentences, the casual confidence. She smiled at Ruthie, her face shimmering under fluorescent lights, her forehead smooth, her reddish-blond hair curving softly under just below her ears. She wore a peach-colored sweater set and pearl earrings. She seemed so, I don't know, so — smart.

Just as I turned back to the tangle of hangers, I heard a *very* familiar voice. "Hey, Mom, there's some Liz Claiborne shirts on the New to Us rack."

Brody. Our eyes met while my arms were entwined in a hanger mobile.

"Hope! Hi. You working here?"

"Well, sort of, not really."

"She keeps the place going," said Ruthie, taking Mrs. Brinkman's clothes to a back rack.

"Mom," said Brody, "this is Hope."

"I'm happy to meet you, Hope," said Mrs. Brinkman with a sparkly white smile.

"Thanks, me too." I tried to return half a sparkly smile.

"Any sweet deals?" asked Brody.

"Sweaters, jackets, turtlenecks, wool pants," I said, dropping my hanger mess back into the box.

Brody nodded. "How's spring break?"

"Okay," I said, wishing I could take another good look at his mother.

"Mrs. Brinkman," said Ruthie, now checking the computer screen, "you have twenty-seven dollars on your account."

"Thank you," said Brody's mom. She smiled at me again. "Hope, could you join us? We're going to play miniature golf."

I didn't know what to say. *Yes, I'd love to play golf with you, dress like you, sound smart like you, live with you.* Geezuz, Brody had an Angel Mom!

"Oh, thanks," I mumbled, "but I'd better not." I looked at Brody. "Maybe another time."

Brody and his mom left with Brody giving me a wave at the front door.

"Ruthie," I said, combing my fingers through my hair, just as tangled as the hangers.

"Uh-huh."

"How do you think I'd look with shorter hair? Like below my ears? I mean, wouldn't it be better for summer?"

"Oh, darlin', you'd look spectacular — let's go for it."

I panicked. *"You're* going to cut it?"

"You think I'm just going to hack away at your lovely hair?" said Ruthie, leading me back to the storage room. "I'll have you know, I was a beautician in my former life."

Before I knew it, Ruthie had me sitting on a stool with a towel from LINENS around my shoulders. She began combing, brushing, untangling, and suggesting shampoos and conditioners.

I rolled my eyes. "Maybe I should just go bald."

"Hold still." She aimed the comb and scissors, poised for attack, then stopped. "What will your mother say?"

"She doesn't care." The words escaped before I could grab them. I panicked. I'd never said them out loud, to anyone.

Ruthie dropped her arms to her sides, her face shifting from happy to sad.

I paused, then slowly said, "She never cares."

"Oh, sweetie, I care." And she bent over, wrapped her arms around the towel, around me, pulling me tight against her chest.

"I care," echoed Anita, walking across the room with an armload of sale signs, "but I certainly wouldn't let this lady near my hair with anything sharp."

"You be nice," said Ruthie, straightening up. "We're about to perform a little magic — just call me the Hairy Godmother."

"Bad, Ruthie, really stinks," said Anita.

"I asked her to," I said in Ruthie's defense.

"Oh, in that case, we're all in trouble." Anita sat at her desk to watch.

Ruthie pressed the cold scissors against my forehead and hair began to fall away. I closed my eyes until, at last, Anita handed me a small mirror. I saw my eyes first. They seemed bigger, browner — prettier. And I seemed older without those long, scraggly ends hitting my shoulders.

"I like it."

CHAPTER 21

The Prize

"Who cut your hair?" Mom demanded.

"It w-was my idea," I stammered. "I asked her and —"

"WHO?"

"Uh, this lady at Next to New. She asked if you'd care and I said you wouldn't."

"I don't," she said, "but the boys will."

"Huh?"

"Boys like girls with long hair."

"Not all boys," I said, wondering if Brody liked his mother's hair short.

Mom threw her hands in the air. "Dye your hair green with purple stripes for all I care."

Sarcasm: 35 points.

The next morning I stood in front of Next to New, checking out my reflection. I touched the soft ends of my shampooed, conditioned, gelled, dried, and curled hair. Thank goodness I liked it after cramping my arm muscles with all that blowing and rolling.

Anita looked up from the cash register. "Ohmygosh. Ruthie! Come see who just walked in."

Ruthie appeared from ACCESSORIES, carrying an armful of belts and purses. "Oh, Hope."

I stiffened.

"It's beautiful," she said, dropping her load right on the floor and marching over to examine me.

I stood there, soaking up all their smiles and shiny eyes.

"Thanks," I said, and without thinking I gave them each a hug and a kiss on the cheek.

Thursday was slow. When we finished our two o'clock break, Anita brought out a cribbage board and deck of cards. "Winner gets a prize," she said.

"I love prizes," said Ruthie. "What is it?"

"You'll see," she said, shuffling the cards.

Cribbage — Anita and Ruthie's favorite game. I'd heard of their nightly matches and a running winner-loser record. At the end of the year, the loser had to take the winner out to dinner in Portland.

I watched as they examined their hands, discarded into the "crib," laid cards on the table, counting as they went, moving little silver pegs into holes around the wooden board.

When Ruthie moved her peg around the last corner, she announced, "Winner! Prize, please."

Anita smiled and took Ruthie's hand, leading her from the storage room to the men's bathroom.

"Excuse me, darlin', but I don't need to go," said Ruthie.

"Come on." Anita tugged.

"The MEN'S room?" Ruthie protested.

Anita didn't answer except for a "Shhh."

I walked behind them and heard a hushed "Ohhhhh."

"Come here, Hope," whispered Anita.

I walked cautiously between them, to a box, peeked over the edge, and smiled. I bent down and watched the gray and white kitten, curled on a bed of towels, stretch a tiny leg forward and arch its head with a slow-motion yawn, then snuggle back to sleep. Its tiny body moved ever so slightly with each quiet breath. I touched its silky fur and began stroking its back. A faint purr floated up from the box.

"Where did you get it?"

"A customer," said Anita, proud of her prize.

I picked up the little fluff ball and cuddled it next to my face.

After more ooohs and aaahs and petting and purring, we named him Resale after vetoing Ruthie's vote for Snickers.

"Looks like you've fallen in love with him already, Hope," said Ruthie. "Why don't you take him home? A companion for Peter."

I froze. "No, no, I couldn't do that." I handed Resale to Ruthie. Please don't ask me why and make me explain that my mother has never allowed pets, that they stink and pee and puke in the house.

"Then Resale will be a shop cat," said Anita, "with Hope in charge." She eyed me. "That means a clean litter box."

I breathed. "No problem." Ruthie placed Resale back in my arms and his little motor began humming.

CHAPTER 22

Preparation & Permission

"Aren't you going to the parents' meeting?" I stared at Mom, stretched out on the couch, watching the news.

"What meeting?"

"*Outdoor School.* I've been reminding you for two weeks." I knew I was getting close to trouble, but I didn't care. This was too important. I held up the flyer I'd taped to the refrigerator. "All the sixth-grade teachers and ODS counselors will be there." My ears warmed a warning but I couldn't quit now. "There's a slide show and refreshments." How else could I convince her!?

"ODS," she said like she was imitating me.

"Outdoor School," I said, verging on angry impatience. "There are important forms to fill out."

"If they're that important, someone will send them to me." She clicked to another channel.

"Mr. Hudson is going to teach some fun campfire songs."

She looked at me. "I don't think so."

"*Please*, Mom. *Please* go. I'll get your jacket and car keys. You just *have* to go."

She sat up. "Hope Marie, stop your damn whining. I don't *have* to do anything." Her eyes narrowed. "And I *do not* take orders from a twelve-year-old."

My arms dropped and the flyer slipped to the floor. I turned and left the living room. The rest of the evening crept by as I stared at my math and out the window. I went to the bathroom and stared at myself in the mirror; I could see the twitching in my cheeks as I ground my teeth back and forth. Maybe Mom would change her mind, get off the couch, and drive to school. She'd be late but that'd be okay. She'd hear the songs and meet the counselors and —

"Hope," called Mom through the bathroom door. My heart jumped. She was going!

"Don't hog the bathroom."

I sighed and watched my eyes droop. "I'm coming." I flushed the empty toilet and ran the sink water.

When I opened the door, Mom smiled and kissed my cheek. "Thanks, sweetie, you saved my life." There it was again, that stupid kissy-sweetie thing right after being so pissy. I hated it. It didn't make any sense and it certainly didn't make me feel kissy-sweetie.

Was this really happening? What I'd dreaded and feared since the first day of sixth grade? That there really was a chance — a big chance — I wouldn't go to Outdoor School? No. It couldn't happen. But I felt like I was sinking into a deep hole, swallowed in cold darkness. *NO*, I wanted to scream, *I'm going!*

The next day, Mr. Hudson gave me a parents' packet. "It has everything in it except the slide show and counselors."

I pulled out the equipment list. Sleeping bag. Air mattress. Flashlight. Suntan lotion. Pajamas or sweats. Boots or sturdy shoes. My sturdy purple boots were ready. So was I. I was going.

*

"I said a **boom** chicka boom." Mr. Hudson clapped his hands and slapped his legs.

"I said a **boom** chicka boom," we called back, clapping and slapping.

"I said a **boom** chicka rocka chicka rocka chicka boom."

Clap, slap, clap, slap. Mr. Hudson looked around the room.

We had pushed the desks against the walls and now sat cross-legged on the floor in a circle with Mr. Hudson sitting in front of the whiteboard.

"Oh, yeah," he said, nodding his head up and down.

"Oh, yeah," we answered, our voices rising, our hands burning.

"One more time."

"One more time."

Outdoor School was still three weeks away, but we were more than ready. We'd learned loud silly songs and quiet nighttime songs, ones with hand motions and some with full-body action, like the "Squirrelly" song where you turn around, bend over, and shake your rear, then hop on one foot in a circle.

We'd learned how *not* to put up a tent when Mr. H wound up in the middle of a green mess.

Now we were making cooking stoves out of empty coffee cans and tuna fish cans. We poked triangular holes around the coffee can base for air vents. Then we made fire starters by rolling narrow strips of ripply cardboard and cramming them into the tuna can, which Mr. Hudson filled with melted wax. As the wax hardened, we stuck a piece of candlewick into the center.

"Buddy burners," announced Mr. Hudson, lighting his fire starter, then placing the open end of the coffee can upside down over the tuna can. He dropped a dab of butter on the flat top of the coffee can stove. The yellow glob sat there for a moment, then eased into a puddle and started bubbling. "There isn't a knob for *high* or *simmer*," he said, spreading the butter with a pancake turner.

We crowded closer as he cracked an egg on the

coffee can edge, then poured the insides onto the buttered griddle. Snapping and popping, the egg quickly changed from slime to a yellow and white eyeball. "You can try for easy-over," said Mr. Hudson, flipping the egg with the pancake turner. He winked at us. "It's in the wrist." With another flip, he had it on a paper plate and handed it to Peter Monroe.

We started to protest but shut up as Mr. Hudson spooned pancake batter on the stove and we all got a turn at flipping and eating.

The next afternoon we pulled all the blinds so the room was dark as a cave. Mr. Hudson turned on his laptop and projector and a bunch of students and parents appeared on the wall screen.

"This is the big ODS sendoff — good-bye for five whole days," he said. "If this is your first time away from home, your mother or father might get a bit teary-eyed. Go ahead and let them. They're just having trouble growing up. Or maybe it's seeing *you* grow up." Everyone except me chuckled politely, like they'd suddenly aged a couple years and were full of sympathy for their poor, sentimental parents.

"These are the showers," said Mr. Hudson, nodding at the small brick building on the screen. "You get one during the week."

"*One?*" someone protested.

"You got it," answered Mr. Hudson. "So, depending on how you want to smell, you may want to pack deodorant." He ignored our giggles.

"You'll definitely need a warm sleeping bag. We've had snow some years." The next slide was a crowd of campers around a snowman wearing an Eola Hills ODS T-shirt.

"And don't forget your counselor's camp name," warned Mr. Hudson as the picture changed. "If you're caught using his or her real name, it's a twenty-five cent fine." Counselors appeared on the screen, stacked in a three-layer pyramid. "Fungus, Cricket, and Gumdrop; Spice and Slug and Mole. They'll all be back this year, so memorize their names."

After the slide show, Mr. Hudson came by my desk. "Do you have your ODS packet, Hope?"

I sighed and inspected the floor. "I can't get Mom to fill out the forms."

"Do you want to go?"

My head jerked up so fast I thought it would snap off and spin across the room. "Are you kidding?"

"Attagirl." Mr. Hudson tapped on the desk with his knuckles. "I'll give your mom a call tonight in case she has any questions."

Each time the phone rang that evening, I inched down the hall toward the kitchen and held my breath. First it was Lydia, then someone for Tyler, then I heard Mom coo into the receiver, "Oh, Mr. Hudson, how very nice to hear from you. Yes, uh-huh. Well, I've just been so busy at work. Uh-huh. Oh, I'm sure it is. I just assumed Hope wouldn't be going since she's such a troublemaker. Oh, really? Outstanding? I haven't seen any pink slips. Uh-huh. Well, I'm sure it's a great experience. No, she's never been camping. I would have volunteered to go, but I just can't get away. Yes, her brother has a sleeping bag. Okay. No, I can't think of anything. Thank you so much for calling, Mr. Hudson. Bye, now." She put the phone down, flipped off the kitchen light, and walked back into the living room.

The next morning I hung around the kitchen, praying I didn't have to beg. Maybe she'd just hand me the packet with a smile and say, *"You're going to have a great time at ODS, Hope."*

"You're making me nervous, Hope, pacing around here like a sick cat." She stood up from the breakfast table. "Go on, catch the bus."

"Did you, are you, umm, could you —"

"For God's sake, Hope, spit it out."

"Outdoor School packet," I blurted.

She rolled her eyes. "I don't remember Tyler hauling so much garbage to and from school." She pushed her chair in. "I've never seen so many ridiculous permission forms."

"What about —?"

She eyed me, her hands on her hips. "You'll get your precious Outdoor Playschool forms."

"When?"

"When I get to it!"

I bit my tongue. 50 points.

CHAPTER 23

The Real Me

I tried to be cool about the whole permission business. I figured Mom was playing some sort of game to make me worry, then she'd fill out the forms at the last minute, and I'd get my ODS T-shirt and pack my bag and climb onto the bus. But the possibility of not going to Outdoor School hung around like thick fog and I went through the next few days in a daze.

"Are you going to Next to New?" Brody asked.

"Huh?"

"Hope, wake up," he said, waving his hand in my face. "You just missed your bus. Are you working today at the store? You know — Next to New."

"No, I don't think so." I looked at him and then

around the school yard. The sun was warm, cutting through my fog, and I smelled the spring-come-summer tang of freshly cut grass. I didn't want to go to the store; I didn't want to go home. I just wanted to do — nothing.

Brody tossed his backpack on the grass. "Race you to the swings." He started running.

"No fair! You got a head start!" I dropped my back-pack and ran after him.

We fell into the black rubber seats gasping for air, hanging on to the cold metal chains.

Brody turned onto his stomach and pushed himself in little circles.

"You're going to get sick," I said, leaning back in my swing, looking at the wide blue sky.

"So are you." He reached over and pulled my chain.

"Hey! Stop it!" I laughed, then we both got quiet, our swings slowing to a stop.

"Do you get along with your parents?" I blurted with-out thinking.

"Yeah, I guess." He leaned down and picked up a handful of rubber pellets.

"Really? You never argue?"

He began tossing the pellets at me. "Not much. Just if I'm watching too much TV."

"I don't think my mom likes me." That whipped right out of my mouth like I had nothing to do with it. I felt like I was watching myself, wondering what I was going to say next.

"What do you mean?"

I hesitated, then felt a closeness to Brody that gave me confidence. Out it came. My crying baby life. Dad leaving. The hurting words. Angel Moms. My closet bed and my point-system notebook.

"Why so many points for *Stupid*?" he asked.

"I hate that word. I hate feeling stupid."

He nodded and was quiet for a moment. Then he asked, "How many points would it be if someone yells from another room, '*Come here!*'? You figure it's really important, or even an emergency, so you drop whatever you're doing and you holler back, '*Coming!*' You race to the next room or downstairs or upstairs, but then you discover they just want to show you something dumb, or have you hold something for a second, or they want to make sure you're not talking on the phone and that your homework's done."

My mind calculated as he rattled on. When he finished, I said, "Three hundred twenty-five points."

He stared.

I smiled.

Keeping my eyes on Brody, I pushed back my swing as far as it could go, my legs stretched up on tiptoe. Then I swung down and zinged past him, shouting, "See how high you can go!"

CHAPTER 24

Grounded

Brody and I raced to touch the sky. We pumped and pulled, our hands gripping the thick chains, our backs flat to the ground, our feet reaching high, higher, then whipping straight down. The air swept against our faces. We laughed as we passed each other, one up, the other down. Once I laughed so hard, drool slipped out of my mouth and smeared my ear.

"Hope Marie." A woman's distant voice.

"Hope Marie Elliot!" Now a yelling voice.

My heart caught. My body stiffened as I strained to turn my head. The turning derailed my downswing and my legs swung the opposite direction as my head. I spotted my mother just as my legs flew back the other direction. My feet banged against the ground and jerked my body to a stop. Brody slowed and stopped. I choked and coughed, my insides threatening to throw up.

"Where have you been?" She stood cross-armed at the edge of the lawn.

I stood up, the swing resting against my rear. "Here," I said, confused and nervous, wondering why she wasn't at work, why she'd come looking for me.

"Is this what you do after school?" She glanced at Brody.

"Well, uh . . ." I stumbled for words, so embarrassed with Brody watching. "Not usually."

Was this a nightmare? Was my mother actually here? Pieces of the puzzle were missing, floating out there, somewhere.

"I have something to show you. Let's go." She snapped around and headed back to the parking lot.

"What happened?" Brody whispered.

"I don't know."

"Are you in trouble?"

"I guess so."

We grabbed our backpacks off the grass and Brody hurried to walk beside me. "Are you going to be okay?"

"Yeah, sure."

"Don't earn a lot of points."

I sucked in a breath and turned for the car. Mom was sitting in the driver's seat. I opened the front door and died.

There, in a pile on my seat, was her blue-and-white-checkered dress. *Oh, God, no. Oh, please, no.*

"Recognize this?" Mom yanked it up and dropped it down.

"Yes," I said weakly.

"Get in."

I fell into the car and pulled the door shut. My face was so hot it stung. *Now what? How bad was this going to be?* The words whirled through my head, over and over.

Now we were passing Next to New. I had to look. There was a naked mannequin in the window.

"I leave the dentist's office and am driving home

when all of a sudden I see *my* dress on *that.*" Mom jabbed her finger at the faceless figure.

I closed my eyes, my heart sinking. "Can I go talk to Anita?" I opened my eyes, hoping to see Mom's nodding head.

She gripped the steering wheel. "We're done talking. We're going home."

We drove in silence. I watched the houses pass. Lawns, windows, trees in pink bloom, kids playing. Did they sleep in their closets? Did they have headaches? Or did they just play and have fun? I shivered and stared at the dashboard.

The car stopped. We were home. I felt myself open the door and follow my mother inside.

"Sit down." She dropped her dress on the kitchen table.

I sat.

"The lady with the dyed red hair said you brought this in. That *I* wanted to sell it. Who the hell do you think you are? Going into my bedroom, snooping through my closet, and *stealing* my clothes?"

I cringed at *stealing*, knowing she was right. I was a no-good, rotten thief.

"What else did you take?"

"Nothing," I said, relieved at the truth. "You never wear it. I thought you didn't want it anymore."

She slammed her hands on the table. "You *thought*. Well, you *thought* wrong. There's no more working at that stinkin' second-rate secondhand store."

I dropped my head.

"You're grounded for the next four weeks."

I closed my eyes.

"And no Outdoor School — that's O — D — S."

My eyes shot open and head flew up. "*NO*, Mom, please, not that! I'll do eight weekends in my room. Ten. All summer. But not Outdoor School. *Please.*"

"You should have thought of that before taking my dress. Now think yourself into your bedroom."

My legs could barely stand with my gut in triple knots.

"And don't even try to change my mind."

My numb feet carried me down the hall, into my

room. I shut the door, saying good-bye to the whole wide world, and saw myself falling again into that dark hole, tumbling, spiraling out of control. My mouth turned watery and my knees wobbled. I stumbled to the wastebasket. My stomach clutched and released, lurched and heaved. Gross. Throwing up in my wastebasket. I waited for a minute, my head still leaning over the side; my body still jerked, but nothing more came up. I sat on the floor, wrapped my arms around myself, and began rocking back and forth, back and forth. *Why me? Why me?* I stared at the wastebasket, my eyes growing heavy, my body still rocking. Sometime later my legs began to ache and I crawled to my closet.

With Turtle tucked under my arm, I slid the door shut. I felt my way under the blankets and nestled my head in my pillow. But sleep wouldn't take me away. Instead, my body tensed from the memory of sharp words and shouting, of threats and punishments.

I clutched Turtle's body, squeezed it tight. Tighter. Then I threw her. She crashed against the closet wall and fell to the floor. Why did I take the dress? What was I thinking? Dumb! Stupid! Idiot!

My eyes stung and my throat swelled. It wasn't fair. Every time I thought things were better, they only turned worse. I'd get my hopes up and then — BAM — shot down! I'd been tricked. Betrayed. Why didn't I run away a long time ago? By now I could be living with an awesome family and going to Outdoor School. Some point system. A lot of good it did me. Like I was ever going to earn the prize. Dumb numbers. Dumb prize. I felt like 1:59. In limbo. Waiting for something to happen, for something to end, to begin, or to get better forever. HA. Like this was ever going to get better.

Exhaustion crept down my body, weighing heavy on my shoulders and legs, yet fighting sleep with sudden jerks and spasms until it finally gave up, gave in, gave out.

The closet door banged open. "You're late."

I squinted at my mother's outline. "I'm sick."

"Liar. You're a thief and a liar. Get going. You'll miss the bus and I'm not driving you to school. I mean it."

Somehow I made it. Tyler managed to prod me along, pouring me a bowl of stale cereal and a glass of sour orange juice. "Brush your teeth," he said, putting my empty bowl in the dishwasher. "Are you wearing yesterday's clothes?"

I shrugged.

"Wash your face — you've got something crusty on it."

I stared at him.

"And comb your hair."

We stood at the corner waiting for the bus, Tyler shifting his sports bag and backpack. "Boyfriend problems?"

I breathed in the cool morning air. A hint of the warming day rode the inhale and I shut my eyes. "No."

"Flunk a test?"

Frustration followed the exhale. "*NO.*"

"What then?"

"What do you think?" I eyed him.

"You and Mom."

"How'd you guess? I'm grounded and no Outdoor School."

"What?" He frowned. "Why?"

The bus stopped and the doors opened.

I looked back at him as I climbed the steps. "I took one of her dresses to Next to New. She found out."

Tyler threw back his head and groaned. "You didn't." He followed me down the aisle and sat beside me. "Geez, Hope, why?"

"You wouldn't understand," I said.

"You can't miss Outdoor School." Tyler leaned against the seat. "You have to go."

Brody met me at the classroom door and followed me to the coat hooks. "What'd your mom do?"

How many times could I say it? Only once more. "I'm grounded, I can't work at Next to New, I can't go to Outdoor School, and I don't want to talk about it." I walked past him to my seat, sat down, and stared at Mr. Hudson's bald spot as he wrote on the board.

The bell rang and someone led the flag salute,

someone read the lunch menu, and Mr. Hudson said something about counselors and wood cookies.

"I'm not sure I have everyone's attention," he said.

I'd been staring out the window. I looked at Mr. Hudson, who was watching me. My face warmed.

"Next week is Extra Credit Week," he said. "If you do a presentation to the class, you'll receive bonus points and something special. It can be on anything we've studied all year." *Points* gave me shivers. Why would I want more points? Besides, extra credit wouldn't earn me the only thing I wanted.

CHAPTER 25

The Pledge

I laid my head on my desk and closed my eyes, longing for my closet. My body ached, like I'd slept on rocks. I remembered waking to strange dreams and bad numbers: 1:13, 2:16, 3:08, 4:57. Each time I woke, I stared into the dark, trying to piece the dreams together.

It started out okay with me as the *Goodnight Moon* bunny, all cozy in my blue-and-white-striped pajamas, saying "goodnight" to the cow jumping over the moon and to the mittens and kittens. But then, the old lady whispering "hush" stood up and pointed her long, sharp knitting needles at me and yelled, "Shut up!" And she wasn't a lady bunny anymore, but a Nazi guard in a blue-and-white-checkered dress with all her fingers chopped off. She only had two thumbs. "Eat your mush," she shouted, "or I'll give it to the mouse and you'll lose your precious bowl forever!"

I madly gulped my mush, choking and coughing, nervously looking everywhere for the mouse, sure he was going to jump right in my bowl. As I swallowed the last spoonful, I threw up all over the green blanket. The old lady started for my bed. I scurried under the sheet and burrowed deep. Safe, I thought. But darkness closed in, my chest tightened, I gasped for air.

I thrashed for the closet light, whacked the lamp shade, then fumbled for the switch. Light, at last, precious light, filling my closet. My body shook in relief and I grabbed Turtle. With my knees to my chest, I rocked back and forth. *Dear God, please help me.*

"Are you okay, Hope?"

It wasn't God. It was Mr. Hudson. And I wasn't in my closet, but back in the classroom, rocking in my chair, my head still on my desk. I swallowed and followed the voice. He was kneeling down, his eyes meeting mine as I turned my head.

"Hope," he said again, quietly, "are you sick?"

"I don't know."

"Do you need to go to the sickroom?"

"I don't know." I stared at his eyebrows.

"What about Mrs. Nelson? Would you like to talk to her?"

"I don't know."

"Come on, let's wander down to her office and see what she's doing." He slowly stood and helped me to my feet. I thought my legs would give out.

"What's up?" Brody came over. "You okay?"

"Yeah."

Mr. Hudson held my arm firmly, just above my elbow, as we walked to the door, and I knew he'd keep me from falling. "I'll be back in a moment, class."

We entered the hallway and I caught a deep breath of fresh air as the third graders headed outside to recess. My legs felt stronger and I stood up straight. Mr. Hudson dropped his hand and strolled alongside me like we were good friends taking a walk together. "Isn't this weather something else?" he said. "Did you hear the thunder last night? It woke my dog and she started howling."

I smiled. It felt good to smile even if I felt miles away.

We stopped in front of Mrs. Nelson's door. "Counselor," it said under her name, and I thought of Dr. McKillip.

Mr. Hudson tapped on the door, then pushed it open. The room was crammed with stacks of books and piles of stuffed animals and puppets. The walls were filled with yellow, orange, purple, and green posters with sayings like "Free to Be Me" and "Let Me Grow in Peace."

Mrs. Nelson looked up from her worktable and set her paintbrush in a glass jar filled with purple paint. Her shiny black hair swept across her shoulders as she stood up. She smiled, her mouth still morning fresh with pink lipstick. I wondered if she had kids and if they got to tell her how they felt.

"What can I do for you two?" she asked cheerfully.

Mr. Hudson put his hand on my shoulder. "Well, Hope isn't sure if she's sick or not, so I thought maybe you could talk to her and see if she needs to go home."

"No!" I practically shouted, then lowered my voice. "I don't need to go home."

Mrs. Nelson looked at Mr. Hudson, her thin black eyebrows raised like McDonald's arches.

"You came at just the right time," she said. "I could use your help with our pledge signs."

Hands & Words Are Not For Hurting stretched across the top of a long piece of white paper. She'd just started the *Pl* of *Pledge*.

I will not use my hands or my words for hurting myself or others. The words floated easily through my mind. They should after six years. Six spring open houses when Mrs. Nelson urged parents and kids to take the pledge, then paint their hand purple, press it to the white paper, and sign their name alongside. Mom figured she'd done it once, so she didn't need to purple up her hand every year.

By the end of the open house, the hallways were filled with purple hands and names. The tiny kinder-gartner hands were so cute with their names spelled with backward letters and long, squiggly tails coming off *y* and *g*, looking like polliwogs.

Mr. Hudson had slipped out of the room and I wondered what I was really doing there.

"Why don't you start at one end of the sign, and I'll work at the other." Mrs. Nelson handed me another jar of purple paint and a brush. "We'll meet in the middle."

I nodded, dipped my brush in the paint, and followed the pencil-drawn *I*.

Mrs. Nelson smoothed the paper at the far end of the table and began writing backward. She didn't break the silence, leaving just the sound of our brushes dipping and tapping against glass, then swishing across dry paper. Quiet is nice. It lets your mind rest.

"So, Hope, how's school going for you?" I guess counselors can't go forever without asking questions.

"Okay, I guess." I kept my eyes on the purple *w*, trying for even curves.

"You guess?" She kept her eyes down, too. "Are you looking forward to Outdoor School?" She moved her paint jar closer to the middle.

"My mom says I can't go." The words sunk in and my stomach rolled. Not go to Outdoor School? Miss the experience of my life? Even snakes? I saw Mr. Hudson the first day of school, peering into our eyes and hissing the word.

"Why not?" asked Mrs. Nelson, as calm as if she were asking why I didn't like cooked carrots.

I shrugged. I knew the answer, but could I tell her? I liked Mrs. Nelson, but I'd already told Brody about Mom. Did I really want the whole world knowing? I concentrated on finishing *will*. "I have headaches."

"So your mom is afraid to let you go because of your headaches?"

"She doesn't care about my headaches."

"She doesn't?"

"No."

"What does she care about?"

"How much things cost."

"She's a single parent, isn't she?" Mrs. Nelson painted away, her questions as smooth as her beautiful brushstrokes.

"Uh-huh."

"Do you remember your father?"

"He left us when I was a baby."

"I'm sorry."

"Me too."

Mrs. Nelson drew the *H* on *Hurting*. I was impressed she could lean her letters together while going the opposite way, like I was always amazed the way Mom could back our car down the driveway and turn into the street just by looking in the rearview mirror.

"How long have you had the headaches?"

I thought for a moment. "All this year, I guess."

"What do you do for them?"

"I wear a mouth guard thing at night so I don't grind my teeth."

"You're grinding your teeth?" Mrs. Nelson set her brush on top of her jar and turned to me. I looked up to see her troubled eyes and pressed pink lips.

"Is that Mr. Hudson giving you too much work?" She tilted her head to one side.

"Not really."

"Are you worried about junior high next year?"

"No."

She stared out the window, like the secret answer to my headaches was floating around the playground.

"What about your friends?" Mrs. Nelson's forehead wrinkled. "Any problems with —"

"It's my mom," I blurted. "We don't get along."

She stepped toward me and reached out her hand, covering my paintbrush hand, soft and warm like a mitten. "I'm so sorry. Do you want to talk about it?" She didn't even notice she'd made me wiggle the y tail.

I stared at her hand.

"Do you know that a lot of students come and talk to me about their parents?"

"No." My eyes stayed on her hand.

"Some kids feel unsafe at home. Some parents yell or scream, hurt others in the family, or throw things, and students come in and share their concerns with me."

I set the brush on my jar and she cupped my empty hand in both of hers.

"Do you feel unsafe at home?"

My eyes went to the window and I studied the third graders swinging and climbing monkey bars and chasing after soccer balls. They seemed happy. Here, anyway. But what about after school, at home? Did they feel safe? Did I feel unsafe? I never thought Mom would hurt me, like burning me with a cigarette like some mothers do. I just felt sick to my stomach whenever I had to go home. Not even Turtle or my closet seemed to help much anymore.

I sighed and looked back at our hands, then at Mrs. Nelson's eyes. "My mother says I'm stupid. And — a dumb shit."

Mrs. Nelson's jaw clamped tight. She'd better be careful, I thought, or she'd need one of those plastic mouth guards. She squeezed my fingers so hard I thought they'd never move again. Dropping my hand, she moved to her desk and sat in her chair. She pulled an orange chair close and patted the seat. "The pledge signs can wait."

She looked out the window again. "Hope, you remember my visit to your classroom?"

"Uh-huh."

"And you know about *hurting words*?"

"Yes."

"That they're *abusive words*?"

"Yes." I didn't think this was a quiz, but I wondered where Mrs. Nelson was going with all her questions. I studied her desk covered with yellow, green, and pink Sticky Notes, lots of them with quotation marks, some with book titles and page numbers. One quote hung crooked from the edge of her computer screen: "No one can make you feel inferior without your consent — Eleanor Roosevelt."

"Does anything else bother you at home?" I'd never seen Mrs. Nelson so serious, and I'd never had this much attention from her. I figured I should try to help her out. I read the quote on her pencil cup: "Albert Einstein's definition of insanity — doing the same thing over and over again and expecting different results." *Over and over again.* Was I going insane? Maybe so.

"I can't seem to do anything right. I try over and over

again but there's always something wrong. I don't do it fast enough or slow enough or good enough."

She glanced at the worktable. "See our sign?"

"Yeah."

"Well, I could have started at the beginning or at the end or in the middle and it would have come out basically the same. Then you came along at just the right time and we started at opposite ends and worked toward each other."

I wondered what this had to do with my mother.

She smiled — finally — then turned in her chair and leaned forward facing me, her arms resting on her legs. "There are many different ways to do the same thing, Hope, and usually they're all just as good. Always keep an open mind about that, would you?" Her strong eyes didn't budge from mine.

I nodded.

Her eyes softened and she spoke slower. "Hope, what do you wish for? How would you change your life if you could? What would make you really happy?"

My skin tingled, my stomach churned, and my heart

beat faster. I felt lighter with each question and wondered if I was about to take off flying, maybe to that tropical island. Any wish I wanted . . . to go to Outdoor School, of course . . . no more headaches . . . no more stomachaches . . . to live with Tyler, Anita, and Ruthie . . . peppermint candy . . . free to say what I wanted to say . . . freedom . . . yes, freedom would make me very happy.

Something broke free inside me, spilling from my eyes, shaking in my voice. A cry rose in my chest and I covered my face with my trembling hands. The muffled words fell in pieces from my lips, through my fingers, breaking apart in the air, "I — want — someone — to — love — me."

I felt arms around me, lifting me gently to my feet; and soft hair against my wet cheeks; a light, sweet whisper in my ear, "It's all right, it's okay"; and a gentle sway back and forth, back and forth.

Mrs. Nelson would probably have kept whispering and swaying all day, but I finally wiped my eyes and sat back in my chair. She patted my knee and waited.

"I'm okay," I said.

She nodded, then cleared her throat. "Hope, if there's any way you can talk to your mother about hurting words, about verbal abuse, it might help." She reached for a pink Sticky Note pad. "Remember, we've practiced *I Statements*," she said as she wrote out an example: "I feel _____ when you _____, and I wish you would _____." She handed me the reminder note. "Look your mother in her eyes when you talk to her."

"I'll try."

"Good luck, Hope. I'll be thinking of you."

"Thanks."

We stood up and she put her arm over my shoulder while walking me to the door. "I feel *good*," she said, "when you *come see me*, and I wish you would *do it more often*."

CHAPTER 26

"I" Statements

I found a pen by the phone and a piece of flowery stationery in Mom's desk. My gut shuddered, but my fingers clenched the pen, found the strength, formed the letters, felt the relief: "I feel *sick* when you *are sarcastic* and I wish you would *say what you're really thinking.*"

Then I set the table with our pretty yellow place mats and matching napkins. I put the silverware out just the right way, with the fork on the left and knife and spoon on the right. I made a pitcher of lemonade and put ice in the glasses and put the note on Mom's place mat.

The note was gone when I returned to the kitchen for

dinner. Tyler was washing his hands in the sink. Grass and mud stains covered his baseball uniform.

"You're not supposed to crawl to the bases," I said.

Tyler casually turned, then flicked his wet hands in my face.

"Ty-ler!" I wiped my face on his jersey and pretended to blow my nose.

He grabbed my wrists and yanked me toward the living room.

"No fighting," warned Mom, setting our plates on the table. "Time to eat."

I glanced around the kitchen, straining to discover even a hint of the flowery note. I tried to sneak looks at Mom's face. She was being way too cheerful, which made me way too nervous.

I suffered through leftover meat loaf and was about to clear the table when she cleared her throat. "Anyone know where *this* came from?" She pulled the missing note from under her place mat and tossed it onto the table.

Tyler read the message, then looked at me. I had no

idea what to do next. *Mrs. Nelson!* I clamped my cold hands together in my lap and tried to look Mom in the eyes, my whole self pleading for her understanding. The wall clock ticked loudly. I slipped one thumb inside my entwined fingers and squeezed it as tight as someone getting a group hug.

"Well," said Mom, picking up the paper, "whoever you are, I feel *you're too sensitive* when I *talk to you* and I wish you would *take a joke.*"

Tyler took the note from her hand and glanced at my once-confident words. "Sarcasm isn't funny, Mom."

She snatched the note back, crumpled it, and tossed it on her dirty plate. "Now I feel *I want to clean this kitchen* and I wish *you would help me.*" She laughed and stood up.

Tyler mouthed to me, "Hang in there."

My body cautiously relaxed. I was relieved I didn't get lectured, but was I losing my mind? Was I really too sensitive? Maybe I did need to lighten up. Was she teasing or was she serious? All I knew for sure was my head ached. Again.

CHAPTER 27

Choices

I struggled with my idea ever since Mr. Hudson reminded us of the extra credit. Just the thought of talking in front of the class gave me the jitters, but *maybe*, just maybe, the extra credit, plus Mr. Hudson's something special, would change my mother's mind about Outdoor School.

I finally decided after Mr. Hudson had talked about control. "Everyone wants to be in control — nations and neighbors, lovers and leaders, mothers and grandmothers, doctors and" — he gave us a little smile — "teachers."

He wrote *control* on the whiteboard.

"There's good control," he said, facing us, "when

people have choices and can pick the path of greatest advantage. There's also bad control, when people cross the path and become demanding, critical, and abusive of others. Somehow they seem to think they're more important than you.

"But," he said, pointing his finger at us, "you don't have to be an abuser; you can choose not to take that path. Nor do you have to be the victim. You always have choices, and the most important one is how you react. You can choose to be strong or choose to give up. You have to tell yourself, 'I am valuable. I am worth saving. I can be free.'

"Remember, you always have a choice over what's up here." He pointed to his head. "And what's in here." He touched his heart.

I felt Mr. Hudson's words all the way down to my feet. No one whispered or wiggled in their seats, so maybe they were feeling his words, too.

"The Hands and Words Are Not For Hurting Pledge is about good control," said Mr. Hudson, raising his right hand. Don't forget to take the pledge again at spring open house and encourage your family to take it, too."

I wish.

It wasn't until the end of the day, when we were putting our chairs on our desks, that I approached Mr. Hudson. "Uh, Mr. H, I'll do an extra-credit report."

He must have been shocked because he just looked at me for a few seconds. Then he quickly gave a thumbs-up. "Good for you, Hope. How about tomorrow, or is that too soon?"

I swallowed. "It's okay."

When Mom came home that evening, I met her at the back door and helped with the Bi-Mart bags.

"I'm doing an extra-credit report tomorrow."

Silence.

"That means I have to get up in front of the class and —"

"I know what it means." Mom pulled out dish soap and coffee filters from the paper bag.

I gripped the back of a chair. "Since I'm getting extra

credit, um, could I" — I paused, then whipped out the words — "could I go to Outdoor School?"

She stared at me, her arms filled with toilet paper and napkins. "Think about it, Hope. What did I tell you?"

I zoned after *think about it*. That told me all I needed to know, but it was too late.

"Answer me, Hope. What did I say?"

My mouth rescued my mind. "You said not to ask."

That evening I sat at my desk with paper, pencil, and pink Post-it notes. I stared at *Anne Frank: Diary of a Young Girl*. How had I gotten the nerve to do a class presentation? I'd even stopped by Next to New to borrow a few things. Anita and Ruthie were all over me, asking about my life, my mom, and saying they were so sorry about the dress business. They, too, hoped the extra credit would change her mind about the store and Outdoor School.

Deep breath. You can do it. *Control, Hope, control.*

I began flipping through Anne's diary, remembering

names and faces, strict schedules, skimpy meals, se-cret visits.

I reread sections, jotted notes on Post-its, and tagged pages. Then I drew a star, colored it yellow, and cut it out.

That night I dreamed again about the *Goodnight Moon* bunny. This time I was trying to rescue him. "Oh!" he said as I tiptoed into the room. "Hush!" shouted the old lady in the rocking chair. The bunny pretended he was asleep, then when she wasn't looking, he whis-pered, "Save the mouse," pointing to the bookshelf. I pointed back at the bunny. He shook his head and pointed sharply to the mouse that was leaning way over the edge of the top shelf. I slipped quietly behind the old lady's rocking chair while the kittens were busy wrestling yarn balls. With a quick snatch, the mouse was in my pocket, and I was out the door.

"Fifteen minutes, Hope, until your presentation," said Mr. Hudson.

In the girls' bathroom, I took off my jeans and pulled out a gray-and-white-striped dress from the Next to New bag. It was too big, going way past my knees, which was perfect. I found the rope-like belt and tied it around my waist. The shoes were mixed — one black and one brown.

I pushed up the left sleeve. With a blue marker, I wrote #8726 on my arm. I pinned on the yellow paper star and looked in the mirror. My heart clenched. I stared at the tired reflection, the drab striped dress, the yellow star. I wavered between past and present, between barbed-wire fences and playground swings, between Nazi guards shouting and Mr. Hudson singing, between brick chimneys and springtime daffodils. Was I coming or going? In Eola Hills or Auschwitz? Fear and relief swept through me at the same time. I shivered with an idea.

Pulling open the restroom door, I stuck my head into the hall. Noelle was coming back from the office with a stack of papers. "Noelle," I whispered loudly.

She paused. "What?"

"Could you bring me a pair of scissors?"

She wrinkled her forehead. "I guess."

When she returned, she stood in the half-opened doorway, staring at my dress. "Geezuz, Hope, what are you doing?"

"You'll see."

She handed me the scissors and left.

I returned to the mirror, took one last look, then grabbed a chunk of hair against my scalp.

With a gray scarf tied tightly around my head, and my clothes in the bag, I walked back to the classroom. My throat was dry and my hands were wet as I opened the door. Anne Frank said she was petrified to go outside. I was petrified to go inside. Mr. Hudson looked up from his desk and the kids around him stared.

"Halloween's not till October," Peter snickered.

"Knock it off, Peter," said Brody.

But it was the whispers and giggles that almost sent me back to the restroom.

"That's enough." Mr. Hudson stood up. "It takes a lot of courage to talk in front of your peers, so let's give

Hope our respect and attention." The whispers stopped, everyone sat down, and I slowly walked to the front of the room gripping my book and notes.

"Hi," I said, my voice shaky. "My name is Anne Frank. I was born June 12, 1929. On Monday morning, July 6, 1942, I went into hiding with my mother, father, and sister. We left our home forever because the German Nazis were rounding up Jewish people like us and taking them to concentration camps and death camps where most of them died of hard work or disease or were killed in gas chambers. We lived for two years in a 'Secret Annexe,' which were some rooms hidden behind a bookshelf in my father's office building. Four other Jewish people lived with us."

I glanced at my notes and cleared my voice. "We had to do many hard things not to be discovered, like not talking and tiptoeing everywhere. Sometimes we couldn't even go to the bathroom."

My voice calmed and the words came easier. "I was scared most of the time. Scared we'd be discovered, scared of the bombs, scared for our friends taken away to work camps where their heads were shaved for lice and their arms tattooed with ID numbers." I pulled up my sleeve and showed my blue-numbered skin.

"It was hard for us to get along with each other, living day after day so close together. People argued over silly things, like the best way to peel potatoes. My own mother made me feel bad, saying things that hurt my feelings. Soon I decided I had only myself to rely on." I glanced at Mr. Hudson, leaning against the back wall. "I chose to be strong. The Nazis had stolen my dignity, and hiding from them stole my few remaining freedoms — to talk and laugh when I wanted, to look out a window and smell fresh air, to eat a decent meal. All I had left was what was in here." I pointed to my head. "I could think anything I wanted without anyone knowing. Without anyone stealing it. And I wrote a lot of it down." I held up Anne's diary, then turned to one of my Post-it note pages.

"I wrote this Thursday, November 19, 1942." My eyes swept the classroom and I was surprised how everyone was paying attention. "'I feel wicked sleeping in a warm bed, while my dearest friends have been knocked down or have fallen into a gutter somewhere out in the cold night. I get frightened when I think of close friends who have now been delivered into the hands of the cruelest brutes that walk the earth. And all because they are Jews!'

"Anne Frank hid for two years before getting caught and sent to a concentration camp. She died seven months later of a disease called typhus. That was over sixty years ago, but we remember her today because of what she said." I set the book and my notes on a table.

"Life is really unfair sometimes and it's hard to wait for good things to happen, but Anne Frank had courage. She played lots of little games to feel in control, like pretending that something was delicious when it was really disgusting. I wish she was alive today so she'd know how important she is."

I reached behind my head, untied my scarf, and slipped it off.

A gasp went through the classroom.

"I gave her the scissors," Noelle said loudly.

Everyone started talking.

"Quiet," said Mr. Hudson, stepping forward. "I don't think Hope is finished."

I waited until they'd settled back in their seats.

"I cut my hair in honor of Anne Frank and the six million victims of the Holocaust."

Everyone started clapping.

"Way to go," whispered Brody as I walked past his desk.

CHAPTER 28

The Last Link

I set the rosebush on the kitchen table. Then I stepped back and studied the smooth tight buds pushing up from the thorny branches.

"*It's believing in roses that makes them bloom,*" Mr. Hudson had said while handing out the extra-credit surprise. "A French proverb that speaks to having a dream, a goal, and working persistently and courageously to achieve it."

When I got my rosebush, he said, "I got the idea from your concentration camp map. I hope you'll take good care of it because that, too, will make it bloom." Brody got one for his report on the underground resistance — people who tried to secretly fight the Nazis.

There were extra-credit maps, science experiments, and special displays, but no other acting.

I leaned my extra-credit grade against the flowerpot. It was on a three-by-five card with these words: *"Remembering Anne Frank by Hope Elliot — A+."* It looked good. No, great. Mom would have to change her mind about Outdoor School once she saw the rosebush and my amazing grade. Then I remembered my hair and my heart sank. I fingered the stubby ends and wondered if Ruthie could salvage what was left.

"I'd never have the guts to do that," Jessica had said after my presentation. "Are you going to dye it, too?"

I almost told her "no," but quickly changed it to "maybe."

"My mom would never let me do that," she said.

"Mine said she didn't care if I dyed it green with purple stripes."

"Your mom is way cool."

My bedroom door opened and Mom leaned against the doorway. "What's with the farm girl look?"

I touched the red bandanna scarf tied around my hair. "Nothin'."

"Who's the rosebush from?" She seemed in a good mood. Probably because I was grounded.

"From Mr. Hudson for extra credit. You like roses, don't you?" I held my breath.

"I don't have time to grow a decent lawn, let alone rosebushes," she said, taking off her shoes. "Why don't you give it to the neighbors?"

"I'm supposed to take care of it myself."

Mom's eyebrows shot up like I had no business taking care of anything. Like I had no clue how to plant, water, fertilize. Maybe she was right. Maybe not.

She turned and walked out. From the hallway came: "Good job on your report." *Good job?* My heart skipped, but my brain interrupted: *Don't get so excited, heart. D.D. probably didn't mean it. Don't set yourself up for disappointment.*

Saturday morning. The phone had rung five times by nine o'clock and someone had knocked at the front door. I hoped the calls weren't from Grandma. That would really put Mom in a crappy mood.

I lay on my closet bed and stared at my hanging clothes, then turned over and buried my head in my pillow. How could I have thought that extra credit and a rosebush would change Mom's mind? Maybe I *was* hopeless. But then I heard Mr. Hudson's voice: "You're not a victim. You have choices."

Right. I have choices. Just like the *Goodnight Moon* bunny, I can look at the ceiling or the walls or my comb and brush. Great choices. I can choose not to go to Outdoor School. My mind went blank and I nuzzled deeper into my flannel pillowcase. But, once again, Mr. Hudson's words intruded: "You can choose to be strong or choose to give up."

I wanted to be strong, but I didn't want to be like Anne Frank, working so hard, hoping things would get better, then losing everything in the end. The Jews should have known it was only going to get worse. They should have escaped at the first signs of trouble.

I sighed. I felt like the sad hum coming from my radio, the singer sending her heartache into my closet. Just what I didn't need, but before I could change the station, the heartache hum turned to heartfelt words. "Broken One, I see you hang your head in shame. Broken One, I see the tears fall like rain, as you try to hide your pain."

I tensed. *Who was that? And where did she find those words?*

"Broken One, you are standing all alone. Broken One, is the pain deep inside or in your home?"

My *home?* My heart paused, waiting for an answer. *Yes,* I wanted to cry into the radio. *Yes, the pain is deep inside, in my home. Who are you, singing words wrapped in such hurt, yet sounding so sweet?* Now her angel voice turned strong and the words sparkled. "I believe there is hope. I believe there is peace. I believe there is love to feel the depth of your soul."

My heart began beating hard as the words rang in my

ears, swept past me, to the top of my clothes and out the closet, filling my room, urging me to get going.

"Take my hand, and I will walk this road with you. Take my hand, and I will carry you through." I sat up. Wide awake.

"I believe there is hope," came the chorus again. *Yes! There is Hope.* My insides shivered. I threw back my covers and sucked in a fresh start.

"Broken One, let your story make you strong as you begin to sing your song. Broken One, find joy once again, and your new life begins."

Maybe, just maybe, I wasn't too tired to do one last thing. I pushed myself up and rocked back on my heels. I found Tyler's sports bag in the back of my closet and opened it on my bed. I *wasn't* going to lose everything in the end. I *was* going to Outdoor School. AND I WASN'T COMING BACK. *There is Hope.*

My purple hiking boots went in the bag first. Then my two pairs of jeans and four T-shirts. Make that five. I tried to remember the list. Underwear and socks. Sweatshirt. That made sense. Toothbrush, toothpaste. I opened my door and crept down the hall, into the bathroom. Washcloth? Towel? I looked through the drawers and medicine cabinet. Band-Aids, sunscreen, mosquito repellent. Yes.

Back in my room, I checked my drawers and closet for anything else. Pj's and my yellow jacket. Flashlight — I needed a flashlight. I ventured out again, this time to the hall closet. The door squeaked.

"Hope, is that you?" Mom's voice came from the kitchen.

"Yeah. I'm looking for something."

"I'm making blueberry pancakes."

"Okay," I shouted back. I grabbed the flashlight, zipped back to my room, tossed it in my bag, and hid the bag in my closet. My knees shook, but I entered the kitchen totally cool.

"What have you been up to?" Mom asked, sitting down across from me.

I tensed. "Uh, cleaning my room. Putting things away."

"I mean at school."

I buttered my pancakes and poured syrup over them. Where was she going with this? "Getting ready for Outdoor School," I answered carefully. "Learning songs, making these little stoves, stuff like that."

"Uh-huh." She lit a cigarette. "Have you made some new friends this year?"

Now she was making me nervous. I knew this wasn't a friendly little mom-daughter chat. It was heading somewhere I probably wouldn't like, but what could I do about it?

"What about some kid named Brody? Weren't the two of you swinging the other day?"

My fork clanked onto the plate and my face turned roasting hot. How did she know his name?

Mom grinned. "I think he likes you." She stood up and walked over to the counter, picked up a round tin, and opened the lid. "Brownies." She brought them to the table. "For me," she said, pushing the lid back on. "He came by this morning. Said he'd heard you were grounded and wondered if the brownies would change my mind about Outdoor School. Made them himself."

Brody had *that* much nerve? Wow.

"Pretty cute kid," Mom was saying. "Dressed like he was going to play golf or something. And his mother, waiting for him in a silver BMW." Mom tilted her head and eyed me. "You've got better taste than I thought."

"How come the phone rang so much this morning?" I asked.

"Your fan club."

"Huh?"

She puffed on her cigarette, exhaled a stream of smoke, then smashed the remains in an ashtray. "I god-damn don't know what the crap's going on, Hope, but I've had enough of this insane parade. First, your principal calls to tell me how important Outdoor School is and how much kids learn in just five days. Then she asks if I have any concerns about the trip." Mom rolled her eyes. "'No,' I tell her. Then Mr. Hudson calls saying I should be very proud of you and your efforts at school. I tell him I'm not exactly proud of your stealing. That shuts him up."

She crossed her arms on the table. "You'd better

stop this right now, young lady." She stared. "You can pass the word that I've made up my mind and not even a mountain can move it."

"I didn't do anything. Honest." I tried to sort it out, but my ears interrupted, beating to my dancing heart, ringing in glorious disbelief: Did all those people *really* stand up for me?

Back in my room, I tried to come up with a plan. I was going to Outdoor School, even if I had to walk. But where would I go after that? A crisis center? Teen runaway house? Abused women's shelter? I'd heard about some places in McMinnville. Yes, that's what I'd do.

Relief rushed through my body, followed by a burst of energy. Lots to do if I was moving out. I started with my closet, throwing away stale saltines, hard Red Vines, and a jar of moldy green olives. I sorted a pile of clothes, folding, hanging, and tossing dirties in my clothes hamper. I washed the dress and scarf from Anita and ironed my new sundress.

When I picked up my pillow to change the case, I saw my point system notebook, hiding there on my flannel sheet. I kneeled down and picked it up. I opened the cover. There was my code list and point values. I hadn't entered any numbers for a while. I don't know if I'd gotten tired of the system, or maybe it just seemed useless. I thumbed through the pages filled with dates and codes and points. At the bottom of each page I'd added the points, and at the end of each month, I had a final total. But I hadn't done a grand total. Quickly I listed the months since it all began, starting in September. My throat tightened as I tallied the numbers: 6,485 in seven months. Pride brought a smile to my lips, pride in all those moments I'd stood silent and had quietly beaten down those hateful words, the *dumb shits,* the *shoulds,* the stares and glares. I'd won. Guido and Joshua would have been proud of me.

My pride quickly faded, however, as I realized I had nothing to show for my hard work. No army tank. No blue ribbon. No gold star. No end to Mom's abusive words. I'd won the game but not the prize.

I walked over to the wastebasket and let my notebook slip from my hand.

I sat on my bed, held Turtle in my lap, and gazed at the wastebasket. Would I yell at my children? Call them *brat* and *stupid*? I'd heard that bad things like yelling and hitting can go down through families just like a bad heart, from mother to daughter, to grandson to great-grandson. Was I going to be a link in that chain? If only I wouldn't forget how the words hurt, how the sarcasm stung, and how the piercing eyes gagged my throat, burned my heart. I lay my head on Turtle's. Would I forget a year from now? Ten years from now?

Slowly I stood up and moved to the wastebasket. I reached down and picked up my notebook. Beneath it was the yellow star I'd worn for my Anne Frank presentation. I looked at both for a moment, then found a glue stick, smeared the back of the star, and pressed it carefully over the black Lab puppy on the front of my notebook. I ran my fingers over the star, feeling each line and point. I wouldn't forget. And I wouldn't be a link.

CHAPTER 29

Saving Hope

The phone didn't ring Sunday morning and no one came to the door. Mom went to a champagne brunch with Lydia. Tyler was at a baseball tournament. I looked through my packed bag ten times, adding more socks and ChapStick and a pair of sunglasses. I wandered around the house, stared out the front window, sat on the couch, went into the kitchen, opened the refrigerator, and studied the orange juice carton.

The telephone rang. I closed the refrigerator door and answered the phone. "Hello."

"Mrs. Elliot?"

"No, this is Hope."

"Oh, Hope, hi, this is Gabriela Feliciano. I'm at Eola High and I —"

Her words faded as I tried to convince myself that it really was Gabriela Feliciano, League MVP and All-State Team — calling *my* house. And not a wrong number. She asked for Mom. But why?

"It's my third year as a counselor, so I'm hoping that will convince your mother."

"What?"

"Convince your mother that she should let you go to Outdoor School," said Gabriela. "I'm going to be your counselor."

NO WAY! "But we don't find that out till the morning we leave."

"Counselors know ahead so we can make wood cookies."

I'd forgotten about our name tags, a competition among the counselors, who decorate the wooden circles with bright paint, tiny beads, and sparkly sequins in amazing designs, then string them on a leather cord.

Cool sixth graders return to school wearing them for the next week or two.

"I'll make you one, Hope, even if you don't get to go."

"I'm going."

"Your mom changed her mind?"

"How do you know about my mom?"

"Oh, we counselors have to know a lot about our campers." Gabriela Feliciano. My counselor. Besides totally awesome and famous, she was super nice and friendly. Now I had to go to Outdoor School for sure.

"Well, then," said Gabriela, sounding relieved about Mom, "I'll get working on those wood cookies and I'll see you soon. Get lots of sleep — the coyotes keep us awake all night."

I could hear the smile in her voice. I couldn't wait. "Thanks for calling."

I was still glowing from Gabriela's call when Mom came home, glowing from too much champagne. She had two dresses draped over one arm and a Next to

New bag in her hand. My mother went into Next to New? Couldn't happen.

"Your lady friends showed up here just as I got home. Anita and Ruby."

"Ruthie," I said, completely confused.

She spread the dresses out on the couch — one silky purple and flowery yellow (cool iron) and the other a red, white, and blue (cotton/steam). "For the Fourth of July." Mom dumped the small sack and picked up American flag earrings.

I smiled, longing to be back at the store, then I braced for Mom's put-down.

"Their clothes aren't half bad." She dropped the earrings and picked up the purple and yellow dress, holding it to her shoulders, spinning around.

I swallowed in disbelief.

"They agreed with me — you shouldn't have taken in my dress without permission. They apologized over and over, saying they should have checked it out." Mom turned in another small circle, the silky dress flowing like flowers in a breeze. "They said I could have fifty percent off anything in the store the days you work there. And they practically wet their pants praising your work and begging to have you back."

The doorbell rang. "My God, stop!" Mom dropped the dress on the couch. "It'd better not be about you."

Please don't be about me.

Mom looked through the peephole then opened the door.

"Hi, I'm Mrs. Nelson, the school counselor at Eola Hills Grade School."

I didn't know whether to cheer or cry.

"I know who you are," Mom said stiffly, "and my answer is still no. Hope is not going to Outdoor School."

"That's fine," said Mrs. Nelson.

What? I wanted to shout. *You're the counselor. You're supposed to make things work out. Your job is to help kids. Don't give up now!*

Mom's shoulders relaxed and she opened the screen door.

"Happy Mother's Day." Mrs. Nelson handed Mom a small bouquet of flowers. "They're from my yard."

Mom held the flowers to her face as if soaking up all their beauty. "Thank you. They smell wonderful."

"I picked them," came a small voice, and a little girl walked right into the house. She grinned and held out a doll. "Samantha helped me."

"Maddie," said Mrs. Nelson, "please say *hello* to Mrs. Elliot and to Hope, her daughter."

"Hello, and Samantha says *hello.*" Maddie waved her doll's arm. "My real name is Madeline, but it's Maddie for short and I like horses. Someday I'm going to have a horse. Or maybe a kitten."

Mrs. Nelson shrugged and smiled at me.

We followed Mom into the living room. Mrs. Nelson's shiny black hair swayed across her pink blouse and Maddie hopped along, the bow on her dress bouncing behind her.

"I'm four," said Maddie, snuggling next to Mrs. Nelson on the couch.

"I'm ten times that old," said Mom, sitting down with a sigh.

"That's old," said Maddie, arranging Samantha on her lap.

Mrs. Nelson rolled her eyes. "Now, sweetheart, I'd like to visit with Mrs. Elliot."

I leaned against the wall hoping to blend in, wondering where this was going.

"We're going to Grandma's." Maddie clapped her doll's hands.

Mrs. Nelson gently touched her daughter's knee. "Maddie, you and Samantha can choose to sit quietly or" — she glanced at me, her face apologetic — "maybe you can visit Hope's bedroom."

Maddie beamed. "I choose her bedroom." She hopped off the couch, hurried to my side, and grasped my hand.

"Well, we didn't exactly give Hope a choice, did we?" Mrs. Nelson laughed.

"That's okay," I said.

"Thank you," said Mrs. Nelson, her words as warm as Maddie's little hand.

As we left the living room, Mrs. Nelson cleared her throat. "Mrs. Elliot, I did stop by to talk about Outdoor School."

My heart clenched and I put my finger to my lips for Maddie to be quiet.

"I respect your decision," Mrs. Nelson went on before Mom or Maddie interrupted. "I'm sure it was difficult."

"No, it wasn't difficult," came my mother's abrupt words.

"Ow, you're squeezing too tight," Maddie whispered loudly, pulling her hand from mine.

"I'm sorry," I whispered back. "Would you like to meet my turtle?"

"Yes!"

I made several trips to the kitchen, getting drinks for Turtle and Samantha and cookies for Maddie, and for any other excuse to hear Mom and Mrs. Nelson.

"She screws up all the time," I heard Mom say. My knees went weak. "The dress was the last straw. She took something away from me; now I'm taking something away from her. Maybe it'll finally make an impression."

I inched to the end of the hall, my heart on hold.

"Why do you think she took it?" asked Mrs. Nelson.

"Money, what else?"

Pause.

"Did she take anything else?"

"No."

Silence.

"Was there something significant about that particular dress?" Mrs. Nelson's soft voice seemed older and more serious than at school.

"I wore it when I brought Hope home from the hospital. There's a picture of us on my dresser."

I prayed Maddie would stay in my room.

"That must have been an amazing day," said Mrs. Nelson.

Right, I thought, *amazingly horrible.*

"Yes," Mom was saying, "a wonderful day."

I froze. *Wonderful?* Did I hear right?

"Does Hope know how you felt?" asked Mrs. Nelson.

"Do you have other children?" asked Mom.

"No, Madeline is our first," said Mrs. Nelson.

"It's a miracle to have a baby, an incredible miracle," said Mom slowly, "but there are a lot of things you never plan on, a lot of things you give up."

My shoulders slumped and my throat tightened.

"Did you have any help?" Now Mrs. Nelson's voice sounded concerned.

Mom laughed. "Are you kidding?"

"I'm sure it's hard being a single mom," said Mrs. Nelson. "But it looks like you've done a great job. Hope is a real joy to have at our school."

"She's got a mind of her own, that's for sure."

"She'll be a good leader," said Mrs. Nelson. "I can see her as an Outdoor School counselor."

I cringed.

"You think I should change my mind, don't you?" Mom asked.

"I think you're in a very uncomfortable situation and I'm sorry you had to make such a difficult decision." I could almost see Mrs. Nelson looking right into my mom's eyes. "But I also wonder if there might be another choice out there, one you'd both feel was more appropriate. Something we've found that works well at school is selecting a discipline closely related to the problem. Is there a consequence for Hope that some-how connects with taking your dress?"

"You mean like ironing my clothes?"

"That's a very appropriate consequence," said Mrs. Nelson. "You catch on quickly."

"Thanks." Mom paused like she was thinking, then she began talking slowly, feeling her way through the new idea. "It would sure get rid of a huge pile, except Hope will probably put the iron right through my clothes."

"No, I won't." The words burst from the hallway into the living room.

"Hope." Mom stood up. So did Mrs. Nelson.

"I'm a good ironer." I walked straight into the living room. "I promise I am. I can iron silk and rayon and cot-ton. I know how to do pleats and ruffles. I can even steam. And I'm sorry about your dress, Mom. But I didn't think you wanted it anymore. You never wear it and I thought it reminded you of all my baby crying, and Dad — and, so" — I choked and felt a rush of tears to my eyes — "so I wanted to get it out of here."

Mrs. Nelson looked like she wanted to run right over and hug me. Mom's hands went to her hips. Panic stabbed my chest. My words had made things worse. Mom was angry at my outburst and now she'd add another punishment. A worse one.

But I had something to say. It was time to break my silence and release the agonizing, lonely hurt. I wasn't sure what to say, though. I wanted my words, each one, to tell exactly how I felt. This was my chance, maybe my only chance. *Please don't interrupt me.*

"Mom." I looked into her eyes and took a deep breath. "I feel sick to my stomach when you call me 'stupid.'"

"Well, I —" Mom started, but Mrs. Nelson put her hand on Mom's shoulder.

"And I feel really stupid when you tell me to 'think about it' and 'repeat what I've just said.'"

"But you stole my dress and tried to sell it." Same old stony voice. She didn't get it. *She didn't get it!* I covered my ears and closed my eyes. *Please, God, please take me away. Anywhere. Just take me away from here.*

Someone touched my shoulders but I didn't open my eyes. I took a shaky breath. "This . . . isn't . . . about . . . the . . . dress."

I opened my eyes and looked at her. With another breath, I said, "I don't think you love me . . . and . . . I'm not sure I love you."

Mom looked surprised — and sad.

Mrs. Nelson squeezed my shoulder and I realized she'd been standing by my side. Her eyes were also sad, but somehow hopeful.

A small hand patted my leg and I looked down to see Maddie holding up Turtle. "She'll make you feel better."

"Thank you," I said, taking Turtle to my chest for comfort and clutching Maddie's hand for strength.

I looked at everyone and suddenly felt confidence in my words. "I've tried to be good," I began again, wiping my eyes on the back of my hand, "but nothing I do ever works. I can't say the right things or do the right things.

I live in my bedroom trying to stay out of your way, Mom. I sneak around, trying not to disturb you. I don't ask for anything or to go anywhere. But maybe that's not enough. Maybe you want me out of here for good. Maybe I should go away."

"You can stay with me," said Maddie. "Mommy, can we go to Grandma's now and can Hope come, too, with her Turtle, and we'll get ice cream to feel better?"

Mrs. Nelson looked like she didn't know what to do next. At school she'd probably lead us in "There's Something We Can Do," but I didn't think she'd start singing in our living room.

"I need Hope to stay here with me." My mother blinked and a tear slipped out of her eye. She stepped closer and placed her hand on top of Maddie's and mine. "I need her here to help me, to iron my clothes."

Great, I thought, *more ironing for my poor arm.*

"And . . ." Mom paused. "Hope needs to pack for Outdoor School."

CHAPTER 30

Hug a Tree

I couldn't sleep. I wasn't cold, not with my long underwear, sweats, socks, gloves, and a stocking hat. Someone was snoring and Jessica's air mattress squeaked
every time she rolled over. I inched quietly out of my
sleeping bag, holding my breath so as not to wake
Gabriela. I mean *Feliz*. That was her counselor name,
meaning "happy" in Spanish, and she called us her
Campistas (campers). Another counselor, Cricket,
named her five kids *Ants*, and Fungus called his boys
Spores.

I crawled to the tent door and slowly unzipped the
canvas flap. Cold air washed my face and tingled my
throat as I breathed in pine trees and campfire smoke.

I curled up next to the opening, forgetting the chill as I took in the perfectly still moonlit campground, tents scattered in a small meadow and along the river, the row of portable camp stoves lined up in front of the kitchen tent, and picnic tables ready for pancakes and pie-iron pizzas.

A million stars danced in the forever black sky and a brilliant yellow star shouted, "Look at me!" If I stared long enough, it turned white, or was it red, or purple? With all the surrounding darkness and stillness, and the giant sky, it seemed I was the only person on the entire earth taking in this magic. It was mine, all mine. But then I had this weird feeling that someone or something was out there, up there in the deep, throbbing heavens, staring back at me, hypnotizing me, urging my body to float up and join the dance.

I was so tired I should have slept like a rock. The past week had been crazy, trying to catch up and get ready. There was a rush of forms to fill out, schoolwork to finish, library books to find and return, and fundraising money to collect. Tyler checked my packed bag and loaned me a sweatshirt and baseball cap plus his flannel sleeping bag. Mom bought a white T-shirt for tie-dyeing and surprised me with a disposable camera. She even got me a packet of three bandanna scarves — red, white, and blue — without a word, a single word, about my chopped-off hair. Can you believe it?

Every time I got a glimpse of Mrs. Nelson at school, I relived her Sunday afternoon visit. I heard every soft word she spoke to my mother and again felt the quiver in my stomach and clutch to my heart as I gathered courage to break my long silence. I wished I could re-member all I'd said, but I'll never forget the lightness that came with my final words, *"Maybe I should go away."* I smiled, thinking of Maddie's confidence and choices and carefree invitation to stay with them. And I clung to the watery shine in my mother's eyes.

"That's quite a brother you have," Mrs. Nelson had said Friday as she tagged my bags in the gym.

"Huh?" Tyler hadn't been home Sunday afternoon.

"Didn't you know?" She looked at me, her eyebrows raised in surprise.

"Know what?"

Mrs. Nelson lowered her clipboard. "Your brother was worried about you. He came to see me last week, concerned about your mother and her decision and how quiet you'd become."

"So you got everyone to call my mom?" I asked.

She shook her head, her ponytail bobbing. "No, Hope, Tyler was the spark. The fire spread by itself. People heard about your situation and wanted to do something. I don't even know who came to your aid."

Mr. Hudson had warned us to leave knives, hatchets, radios, and hair dryers at home. We were to bring everything Friday so the truck would be ready for our seven o'clock departure Monday morning. "Just bring a sack lunch," he said. "Tofu surprise and liver sandwiches are excellent." No comment.

After a long bus ride singing loud songs and waving at passing cars, we'd hiked into camp, unloaded the U-Haul and two pickups, pitched our tents, and were assigned camp duties. I helped clean the girls' bathroom — a small brick building with damp concrete floors and cold running water. There were funny mirrors above the sinks, some sort of smooth metal with faint, wavy reflections. I guess we wouldn't want to see ourselves, anyway, in a few days.

Something rustled now in the brush and I strained through the tent opening, the moonlight and shadows, to see a deer move cautiously to the stoves and worktables, sniffing the ground and flicking her ears. When she finished her inspection, she glanced around, then wandered slowly between the tents and across the river.

The next morning before breakfast, Jessica leaned over and whispered in my ear, "Squid and Cougar are *too* cute." I followed her gaze to the high school counselors revving their campers to sing loudest for breakfast.

"Okay, gang," shouted Eagle Eye (Mr. Hudson), "let's

see who's going to line up first." He started singing, "There was a desperado —"

"From the wild and woolly west," we all chimed in, shouting our early morning best.

"Gumdrop's group goes first," Eagle Eye announced after voting with the other sixth-grade teachers, Miss Lindquist and Mr. Richmond. The rest of us protested, claiming horrid hunger pains.

Gabriela, uh, Feliz, corralled us in line. "Next time, we're first," she said, her arm draped around my shoulder.

"Yeah! All right!" we shouted.

"Who's number one?" she called out.

"*Campistas!*" we answered.

"*Rattlers!*" came a chorus from Snake's kids.

Settled at our table, we dived into sausage, scrambled eggs, and cinnamon rolls. I shook my milk carton, but it was frozen. "Do this," said Feliz, banging it on the wooden table. We all drummed away, then slurped out milky crystals.

After breakfast and camp cleanup, we split into study

sessions. Some headed to the fire pit to learn five kinds of fire making, then cooked Hunter's Stew in the coals. Others did water testing from the Deschutes River, or learned about the plants and animals of Central Oregon. My tent group was in Frog's survival-skills class.

Jessica was the only one from Mr. Hudson's class in my group. Shawna Gilson had been in my fourth grade class, but I'd never been around the other two, Jenny Nyberg and Ellie Hoyt. They were best friends and didn't talk that much to the rest of us.

We sat around a picnic table with Frog standing at the end. "Ribbet," he said. "That means 'hi, how are you doin'?' in frog talk." We giggled and Shawna answered, "Ribbet." We giggled again.

He ran his hand through his black hair. "Okay," he announced, his thick eyebrows bobbing up and down. "Let's see what we've got here." He unzipped a backpack, then looked at us, getting all serious. "Anytime you head out on a hike, remind yourself that you could get lost and you could spend the night outdoors. Do you know the first rule if you get lost?"

No answer.

"Admit you're lost."

"Hi, tree, I'm lost," said Shawna.

I looked at the pines, their tops glowing warm in the morning sunlight.

"You can talk to the trees all you want," said Frog, "but be sure to hug one."

"And kiss it?" said Ellie Hoyt.

"Yuck," said Jenny.

"Hug a tree means to stay put," said Frog, pulling things out of his backpack. "Don't wander around trying to find your way out. Searchers will start looking where you were seen last."

Across the table Frog had lined up a pocketknife, a film canister housing waterproof matches, a plastic garbage bag, a whistle, a mirror, granola bars, and a water bottle. After explaining why we needed them in a survival kit, he gave us each our own whistle, then led us into the woods. We picked our tree to hug and Ellie really did kiss hers. Then we gathered leaves, grass, moss, pine needles, and dead fern fronds. Frog pulled the plastic garbage bag and pocketknife out of his backpack. "Let's say Hope is lost." I almost fell over at the sound of my name. I swallowed and my eyes zeroed in on Frog.

He motioned me to his side.

"Kiss a tree," said Ellie.

I moved to Frog's side, feeling honored to be lost.

Frog opened the pocketknife and cut a hole in the bottom of the garbage bag. "In you go," he said, and I slipped inside the bag, my head popping out the hole.

Everyone applauded. I bowed.

"Now, let's make sure Hope stays warm for her long night in the woods." He motioned for me to lie down on the ground and began filling my bag with our forest gatherings. "Hope needs a little insulation." I groaned. With great fun, everyone crammed pine needles and leaves and other dead things into my bag.

"The Abominable Snowman," Jenny announced.

"Snowwoman," said Shawna.

"I feel like a stuffed turtle," I moaned.

"Everyone — kneel down around Hope," instructed Frog, holding his camera.

Ellie whipped her fingers behind my head. "We're lost, come find us," called Jessica. But I didn't feel lost at all — I felt unbelievably found.

Shawna blew her whistle.

"Say 'we're hungry,'" answered Frog.

"We're hungry," came the chorus, and the camera clicked.

CHAPTER 31

What Is the Tie That Binds Us?

One day melted into the next, a blur of campfires and counselor skits, soggy French toast and sticky s'mores, table lashing, knot tying, banana boats, and map and compass games.

We learned that Newberry Volcano covers five hundred square miles and the five-mile-wide crater contains two lakes and a lava flow of black glass called obsidian. Hiking up Lava Butte, we followed a twisting path cut into steep lava flows. (My purple boots were awesome.) At the top we could see the snow-covered Cascade Mountains stretching south toward California and north into Washington.

We learned to tell the difference between heatstroke and sunstroke; between ponderosa and lodgepole pines; and between skunk, coyote, and whitetail deer tracks. At Wizard Falls Fish Hatchery, a volunteer named Art showed us how nearly four million eggs hatch each year and become releasable fingerlings. We learned that feeding a tankful of fingerlings is way more exciting than sprinkling your goldfish bowl with those dried, pale-colored flakes. When you toss these specially made fish-guts nuggets into the concrete holding tanks, thousands of calm fish go crazy, thrashing in every direction, breaking the surface, churning the water like a giant blender. Afterward, we hit the restrooms, furiously scrubbing our stinky hands, before touching our lunch.

Other important things we learned: Peter was a sleepwalker and Noelle knew how to rappel because her uncle climbed mountains. Colin Davis recognized edible plants because his mother and grandmother had been Camp Fire girls. And Justin Thayer could really wiggle his tail. That's because he was always leaving his stuff around and had to sing the "Squirrelly" song to get it back. "Squirrelly, squirrelly, shake your bushy tail," we'd sing to him as he stood in front of the lunch line with other forgetful campers, turning and shaking their rears.

I learned that someone, not to be named, wet his/her sleeping bag, and that someone else, not to be named, was so homesick he/she threw up.

One night at campfire I learned that Brody could sing. We were sitting next to each other on this big log and the song we were singing wasn't a shouting one, so I could hear his voice.

"In a cavern, in a canyon, excavating for a mine, dwelt a miner, 'forty-niner, and his daughter, Clementine."

It was nice hearing someone sing in tune, except I couldn't get the words out of my head the next day. And guess where we went? The Lava River Cave — down into this pitch-black cavern with small flashlights swinging around our necks, feeling like miners searching for gold. Counselors held big lantern flashlights and we started out in groups with lots of room between the cold, wet walls and drippy ceiling.

"Ohhh, wow, look at that," said Shawna, shining her light on a sparkling silver wall.

"It's bacteria from soil that's filtered down through the cave ceiling," said Feliz, moving her flashlight around the wall. "And a chemical reaction to your light causes the sparkle."

Gradually we found ourselves squishing closer together and lowering our heads, then going single file.

"We're near the end," came the warning. Mr. Hudson had explained how the cave gets so small at the very end that you have to crawl. If you want to touch the very, very end of the cave, you have to lie down on your back and push yourself feet first through this narrow opening, point your toes, and stretch your hardest. I already felt a little clammy and queasy, and I'd bumped my head twice on the hard ceiling, but my gut told me I had to do it.

When it was my turn, Mr. Hudson helped me get into position. "Okay, Hope, finish it."

With my arms kinda shaky, I managed to push forward. *Come on, come on, wall, hit my toes.* It seemed like forever, but then I felt the nudge on my left foot. One more push and my right foot touched. "Got it!" Everyone hooted and hollered and something bright and tingly rushed from my head to the tips of my purple boots. But as I inched myself back out, something very different and strange gripped my gut, something like hunger, but not a food kind of hunger. I suddenly wanted my mother there. I wanted her to be proud of me.

Back at camp it was my day for a shower. Four days without one and I had to stink, but all I could smell was smoke and I liked that smell. I stood in the stream of hot water pouring off my head and down my back. This was our last night. I'd tried to put it out of my mind all day. One last campfire, one last round of skits. I hoped Mr. Hudson would do another one. He was hilarious in the makeup skit, where he was a woman wearing this wig and big shirt, and someone else, hidden behind him, slipped their arms into the shirtsleeves and tried putting makeup on him. Since the hidden person couldn't see, lipstick ended up on Mr. Hudson's nose and eye shadow on his chin and mascara on his forehead. When they were finished, Mr. Hudson looked in a little mirror. "Oh my," he said in this high squeaky voice, "how lovely!"

Walking back to my tent from the shower room, I felt incredibly clean, smelling of apple shampoo and peach conditioner. I passed the tie-dye trees — limbs covered with soaking-wet orange, green, and purple T-shirts, drying ahead of the nighttime frost. The parent volunteers were making our last dinner. Litter patrol was wandering between tents, and wood gatherers were hauling the last load of dead twigs and rotten sticks to the fire ring. I paused in front of my tent, removed my shoes on the little piece of muddy carpet, stepped past the sun-bleached gray flap, into the heavy odors of flannel sleeping bags and smoky clothes, sweaty socks, and damp towels. Jenny's aloe vera gel had oozed onto the tent floor and her banana-scented sunscreen gagged the air, but I already missed it.

At campfire that night, Brody's tent put on a skit called *J.C. Penney.* "Where'd you get your hat?" their counselor asked Peter. "J.C. Penney." "Where'd you get your shirt?" Peter asked Trask. "J.C. Penney." "Where'd you get your shorts?" Trask asked Seth Jacobs. "J.C. Penney." In walked Brody wearing only a towel. "I'm J.C. Penney," he announced.

"You go, Brode!" someone shouted.

The parent volunteers sang a song they'd made up about all the counselors. Then Eagle Eye gave out camper awards for the most adventurous, the best fire builder, the fastest shower taker, the loudest singer. My name was called for best spelunker — that's a cave explorer. I got a ribbon and a hug.

"This is our twenty-third Outdoor School," said Mr. Hudson, when he'd finished the awards, "and I have to say one of the very best. You were great campers, eager to learn and willing to help. The weather cooperated, except for that one afternoon rainstorm." We laughed, remembering the surprise "shower" we gave Mr. Hudson as he climbed off the bus from the Metolius Headwaters trip.

"I expect you'll all return home tomorrow a little bit changed. How?" He shook his head. "I can't answer that, but for the better I'm quite sure." He looked up at the sky. "Before you go to bed tonight, I'd like you to make a wish for a camper next year — that he or she will have the same wonderful experience you had this week."

We formed our nightly friendship circle, crossing arms and holding hands, stretching wide around the campfire. "What is the tie that binds us," Eagle Eye began and we joined in, "friends of the long, long years? Just this — we have shared the weather, we have slumbered side by side, and friends who have camped together shall never again divide." We sang taps, gave each other's hands a sharp squeeze (the boys always gave torturous clamps, but we girls refused to utter a single peep), then walked to our tents for the last time. I searched the Central Oregon night sky, found the brightest yellow star, and made a wish for a future camper. I added a P.S., a wish for myself, that I'd come back again someday — as a counselor.

CHAPTER 32

A New Beginning

The next morning, after blueberry pancakes and hot chocolate, we rolled our sleeping bags, swept our tents, and broke them down and packed them up. After stuffing the U-Haul and cleaning the bathrooms one last time, we posed for pictures: all-camp, tent groups, combinations of new camp friends, shots of the counselors in a giant, teetering pyramid, and the parent volunteers standing in front of the U-Haul. Jenny, Ellie, and I got Frog to hug a tree with us. Feliz took four pictures. We autographed each other's journals, T-shirts, and jeans. Then we piled into the buses, shouting out the windows to the parents and waving to anyone who'd wave back.

The buses crawled out the rutted campground road and crossed the Deschutes.

I leaned my head against the window frame. Good-bye river. Good-bye meadow and campfire, good-bye frozen milk and burned marshmallows. Good-bye. My chest ached and my shoulders suddenly felt very heavy. I closed my eyes.

The bus stopped. My neck was bent in half, my chin pressed against my chest. Slowly I untangled my body and looked around. Most everyone was asleep, leaning on their neighbor's shoulder, or with their head back, mouth opened. Hats were tilted, hair uncombed. Legs and arms slopped into the aisle. Wood cookies dangled every which way.

Almost home, I thought. My jaw tightened and my teeth ground together. I'd forgotten to wear my night guard at camp, but my headache had disappeared. Was it coming back? Please, no, not the headache. We'd problem-solved all week, but they were fun problems like starting a one-match fire or marking a trail. The thought of bad problems to solve sent pangs of panic through my body. I was wide awake now, staring at the outskirts of Eola Hills, wishing we could turn around, go back, begin the week over.

Moans and groans filled the bus as we stopped again. I peered at the bank temperature-clock. 78 degrees. 4:56. I hadn't seen a wristwatch or clock in five days, which was fine since I'd given up on numbers. But these were pretty good ones. Great, in fact. I kissed my fingers, touched the window, and wished it was a good sign.

We turned the corner and drove two more blocks to the school, all the while my body tensing, my breath waiting, my eyes alert. Cars and pickups filled the parking lot. Parents chatted in small groups while younger brothers and sisters played on the swings and slides. I searched the parking lot with half of me hoping and half fearing. Then I spotted Mom's car and my heart jumped. I hadn't been forgotten.

When the bus stopped in front of the covered play

area, no one moved. "Come on, campers, we're home," said Miss Lindquist. Slowly we gathered our backpacks and extra blankets, hats and crumpled sack lunches. I fell in line, watching as parents greeted their sons and daughters with wide smiles and strong hugs. My throat tightened and my ears warmed. I stepped off the bus and someone moved out of the crowd.

"How are you, sweetie?" It was my mother's voice, but I barely heard. All I could do was stare at the blue-and-white-checkered dress.

With questions spinning like a roulette wheel, one finally settled on my lips. "Why are you wearing that dress?"

"Well," Mom said, "you came home for the very first time with me in this dress, and now you've come home again."

This had to be a dream.

We walked in silence to the soccer field where the U-Haul had parked. I didn't know what to say next, and I was afraid I'd break the spell.

We found all my stuff, and while Mom held Tyler's sleeping bag, I gave a final good-bye hug to Gabriela.

"I've been really busy while you were gone," said Mom as we headed for the car. "I went through all my clothes and took a bunch of things into Next to New. Anita thought I could make some good money. Tyler's baseball team is in the playoffs. There's a game tomorrow in Gaston. Maybe you'd like to go."

We stowed my things on the backseat and Mom asked about Outdoor School. I started slowly, but before I knew it I was rattling on about the crazy counselors and banana boats, river walks, compass hikes, and my award. I explained Mr. Hudson's makeup skit and we both started laughing.

"And when I'm in high school I'm going to be a counselor and I think my name will be —"

"What *are* you thinking, Hope?" Mom interrupted. "A counselor? Responsible for all those children?" Her voice pounced on the words. "You haven't even started babysitting. You won't possibly be able to —"

Wham! My mouth slammed shut, my words rear-ending each other. My head fell back against the seat and I closed my eyes. *Don't go there, Mom. Please, don't do it. Stop. STOP. I can't handle it. Not now, not after this week.* My heart beat so hard it hurt. *I know happiness and I won't trade it in. No, I won't. I choose to be strong and free. I believe in roses. I believe in hope.*

At the next streetlight I'm getting out and running back to the school. Gabriela will still be there for me and she'll take me home with her. Forever.

"Hope. Hope." The car had stopped. We were parked along the sidewalk. *I could jump out right now, grab my bag off the backseat, and —*

"Hope." Mom's hand was on my knee. With her other hand she was offering me a Kleenex. I took the Kleenex and slowly wiped the tears from my cheek.

Mom moved closer and put her arm around my shoulder. "I'm sorry, Hope. I didn't mean that. I — I'm —" She closed her eyes and I could feel her arm trembling through my T-shirt. "I'm taking Mrs. Nelson's parenting class." She laid her hand on top of mine. "I've already gone twice this week."

Her hand was warm and her bare arm felt soft on my neck. I didn't know what to say, and it seemed she was trying to come up with something else.

"I love that dress." She pointed out the window. We were parked in front of Next to New. The mannequin in the display wore an airy chiffon dress covered with pale green, pink, and lavender flowers splashed together like a painting. The V-neck was lined with a floaty ruffle that went down the front, then scalloped along the hem.

"We're having a Southern Plantation party at work next Friday and we're supposed to dress accordingly."

I strained to see inside the store but couldn't get past the dreamy dress and backdrop.

"Any chance you can work here before Friday so I can get it half off?"

I stared at the dress and words spun in my head. *Parenting class. Twice a week. Work. Next to New. Dress. Parenting class.* My jaw relaxed and somehow the words came out. "I think so."

When we drove into the garage Mom turned off the car, but I couldn't move. My body that had hiked and climbed and crawled and sang and shouted had quit on me.

"Come on, let's get you inside before you fall asleep." Mom got out of the car and opened the kitchen door. I followed, banging my bag through the door, dropping it on the floor next to the table.

"I mixed a pitcher of lemonade," Mom said. She moved to the refrigerator and I about fainted. There, on the refrigerator door, was purple paper with Mom's out-lined hand, her name signed and dated. She'd taken the pledge! I tried to imagine it: Mom standing in a classroom with other parents, raising her hand, and saying, "I will not use my hands or my words for hurting myself or others."

I fell into a chair, laid my head on my folded arms, and smiled. Maybe I'd sleep here tonight.

Ice clinked in the glass as Mom set it in front of me. She sat down across the table. "I watered your rose-bush while you were gone."

"Thank you." *Please, God, let this be for real. Please.*

"We should plant it, don't you think? Maybe by the front door? Or do you like the back door better?"

Panic. If I planted my rosebush, then I'd have to dig it up if I needed to leave in a hurry.

"Hope?"

I settled my chin in my hands and looked at her. She was pretty in the blue and white dress. And I hadn't noticed until now she'd cut her hair. Not a lot, but I could tell.

She took a sip of lemonade. "Hope, I need to tell you something."

Alert. Alert. People give those warning words just before saying something bad. I sat up straight. "What?"

Mom ran her fingers up and down the drippy sides of her glass. "I told you I'm taking this parenting class."

I stared but Mom was focused on her drink.

"I've never done anything like this before. I always thought parenting was supposed to come easy, like riding a bike. You have a baby and, bingo, you automatically know what to do. Well, being a parent's a lot harder than riding a bike, and I've fallen off a few times."

She looked at me with sorry eyes. "Hope, I really missed you while you were gone. I know I've said things that have hurt your feelings, but I didn't know how to stop. Sort of like people trying to quit smoking or drinking." She took a deep breath. "Anyway, what I'm trying to say is, I think this is going to be really hard for me. Mrs. Nelson's giving us lots of new stuff and I think it'll take me a long time. You know," she said, chuckling, "old dogs and new tricks." Now she looked at me, sort of worried. "I'll need your help."

My help. She'll need *my* help?

Then I had an idea. I pushed out my chair and stood up.

"Don't go." Now she really did look worried.

"Just a sec, I'll be right back." I zipped down the hall, opened my bedroom door, crawled across my bed and into my closet, reached under my pillow, and pulled out my point system notebook. I paused, then slowly, carefully, tore out my pages of numbers and symbols. I tucked them back under my pillow, pulled out the little bits of loose paper in the metal spiral, then hurried back to the kitchen.

Mom was still at the table and I set the notebook down in front of her.

"What's this?" She picked it up. "Scratch paper?"

"No. It's a special book. To help you get through this parenting thing."

Now she looked confused.

"See," I said, grabbing a pencil, "you give yourself points for doing a good job. Take the word *stupid,* for instance. You really don't want to call me that. So if you catch yourself, even if you say the *st* part, it's still not too late. Then you give yourself points, say two hundred, and maybe one hundred for not saying *brat.*"

I wrote down the date, the letters *S* and *BR,* and next to them 200 and 100.

Mom studied the page, flipped through the note-book, then closed it. "Good idea, Hope."

"Thank you." Was my heart going to break? "And you get one hundred points for telling me 'good idea.'"

"But what do I do with all the points?"

"You get to choose. Something special."

Mom's face relaxed, like she was already thinking of her prize. She ran her fingers over the cover, outlining the yellow star. "What's this for?"

As I gazed at the yellow star, I thought of Anne Frank and the starlit nights she watched from her secret hiding place. I thought of the Holocaust victims, branded with the yellow star because of their beliefs. I remembered the sparkling sky covering our campsite and last night's wishing star. I looked my mother in her eyes and said, "So you'll never forget."

Hope Notes

1. When you're too tired, confused, or frustrated to come up with a big plan, start with a small one.

2. When something's bothering you, talk to someone you trust, like a teacher, coach, or friend.

3. Fix up a special place that's all your own.

4. When everything goes wrong, find something to laugh about.

5. Remember the good times.

6. Join a team or club.

7. Keep trying. Don't give up.

8. Rain or shine? You decide.

9. Find a way to express your feelings, like writing in a journal or making up poetry or painting.

10. Make friends with people who listen without interrupting.

11. Learn more about verbal abuse on the Internet or at the library or local bookstore.

12. Stand up to verbal abuse. Help organizations that promote good relationships such as the Hands & Words Are Not For Hurting Project (*www.handsproject.org*).

13. Look for a verbal abuse support group, or help start one.

14. "I feel statements" don't usually work with verbal abusers. The abuser is often *glad* you feel *sad*. Ask your school counselor or another adult whose advice you trust to offer a different suggestion. One idea would be to take a stronger approach, saying something like: "I don't want to be with you when you hurt my feelings."

15. Call the Childhelp National Child Abuse Hotline: 1-800-4-A-Child (1-800-422-4453).

16. Give yourself gold stars, points, prizes, rewards, pats on the back. (We're never too old for star charts.)

17. Believe in yourself.

18. *Love yourself.*

❈ ACKNOWLEDGMENTS ❈
Call Me Hope

Thank you to my writing colleagues, Sharon Michaud and Kathy Beckwith, who painstakingly read countless revisions, offered wise suggestions, and passionately supported my dream for children to recognize verbal abuse and its devastating impact.

Deep appreciation to Patricia Evans, author of numerous books on verbal abuse, but especially for *The Verbally Abusive Relationship*, which opened my eyes and ears to the covert subtleties of this oppressive condition.

Thanks to Pat Stanislaski, former director of the National/International Center for Assault Prevention, who read an early draft for accuracy and offered the approval I needed to continue.

To the staff and students at Amity Elementary School, particularly fifth-grade teacher Jeff Geissler and counselor Marie Roth for graciously hosting numerous visits, answering endless questions, and reviewing the manuscript. Many thanks to others who took time to read and comment: Lauren Andreassen, Linda Ballard, Ginny Gardea, Melissa Hart, Susan Powell, and Bev Willius.

I am indebted to Carole Fewx, co-owner of Jackson's Books in Salem, Oregon, who introduced me to sales representatives at the Pacific Northwest Booksellers Association Tradeshow, and to Randy Hickernell for sending my proposal to Little, Brown and Company Books for Young Readers.

Enormous gratitude to editor Alvina Ling, who saw potential in that proposal and subsequent manuscript, then gave me the opportunity to revise. She pronounced it a "worthy project," presented it to the editorial staff, pitched it to the acquisitions committee, and offered me a contract. With a gentle touch, she guided me through the ensuing stages to this heartfelt creation.

Thanks to Alvina's assistants, Rebekah McKay and Connie Hsu; to copyeditor, Kerry Johnson; editorial director, Andrea Spooner; designer, Alison Impey; publisher, Megan Tingley; and to the entire editorial department for supporting Alvina and our project.

A published book can't go far if no one knows about it, so sincere thanks to the marketing department for spreading the word.

I am eternally grateful to Ann Kelly, founder and executive director of the Hands & Words Are Not For Hurting Project. Her incredible insight, compassion, and tireless work in the field of abuse and violence prevention will truly make this world a better place. Thank you for every piece of this program, but particularly for the pledge of hope and personal accountability that is changing and saving lives. Thank you for "The Power of One" and entrusting me with your message.

Thank you to the following research resources: Paul Kopperman, Oregon State University professor of history and chair of the OSU Holocaust Memorial Committee; Jerry Moe, national director of children's programs at the Betty Ford Center for "Name it and Tame it"; Josh Isgur, program coordinator at the Washington State Holocaust Education Resource Center; and volunteers in the Juliette's House Safe Kids Program.

I am especially grateful to a man of courage, sensitivity, and inspiration — Alter Wiener, Holocaust survivor.

❋ Call Me Hope ❋
READER'S GUIDE

1. Hope hates to be called "hopeless," "loser," "brat." What are some names that hurt your feelings? Hope gets "one stinkin' stomachache" when her mother says she's "stupid." How does your body react when someone says something hurtful to you? When someone says something nice to you?

2. How do you think Hope's Point System (p. 58) helps her? Do you think it works? Make up your own point system. When would you use it?

3. Why do you think Hope feels so safe and peaceful in her closet hideaway? Do you have a special place all your own? Explain why it's so special. If you don't have such a place, describe where and how you might create one. What would you put in it?

4. When Hope's mother makes her feel bad, Hope turns to *The Diary of Anne Frank* and the film *Life Is Beautiful.* How do you think Hope's home life compares to the long list of restrictions placed on the Jews? (p. 14) If she could travel back in time, what advice would she give to Anne Frank? Compare Hope's situation with Joshua's in the film *Life Is Beautiful.*

5. The frog story (p. 110) illustrates how we gradually become used to hurtful words and actions, but they are still extremely harmful. Give an example of the frog story, either in *Call Me Hope* or in our own day-to-day lives.

6. When Hope sees the purple boots, she knows immediately that she has to have them. Why do you think the purple boots are so important to Hope? Do you have something that's very important to you? Why is it your favorite object?

7. Why is Hope's mother verbally abusive to Hope but not to Tyler? If you have siblings, are you all held to the same rules? How does it make you feel when you're treated differently by your family? If you don't have a sibling, do you feel like you would be treated differently if you did have a brother or sister? In what ways do you think life would be different?

8. Hope receives comfort and strength from many people in her life, such as her friends at the store, Next to New. Who do you think gives her the most help? Why? Whom can you talk to at school, in your family, or community who listens and supports you?

9. Hope's favorite photo is the one in which her mother is holding her as a baby and wearing a blue-and-white checkered sundress. Why do you think Hope takes this sundress? Do you have a favorite photo of a special occasion or of yourself? Explain why you chose it.

10. What would be your strategy to share the Hands &
    Words Are Not For Hurting Project® with others?

11. When Hope sorts through her clothes, she donates
    some to a charity. What possession haven't you
    used in a year? Who would appreciate receiving it?
    If you had one hundred dollars to give to someone
    else or to a charity, who or what organization would
    you choose and why?

12. At the end of the book, Hope's mother is trying to
    change. Do you think people can change? Become
    nicer? More caring?

13. What does the word "hope" mean to you? Read "Hope
    Notes" at the end of the book. Add your own ideas.